"I'm your man."

She laughed. "Actually, I'm your woman. I'm here if you need someone to talk to. In the past few weeks you've let me be me more than anyone else ever has. Only fair to return the favor." She leaned back on the picnic table, stretching the fabric across her breasts. "And the best part? Once we go back to our lives, we'll probably never see each other again. But even a momentary connection is better than nothing."

He had a feeling there was an underlying meaning to that last part. "Are we still talking about...talking?"

Emily turned to him, giving him a glimpse of gorgeous leg.

"This is me going with the flow." She drew in a deep breath. "Seizing the moment."

"Being reckless."

"That, too. But the great thing about knowing what the possibilities are—or aren't—from the get-go is that there are no expectations. So you can relax and enjoy the moment."

His blood pumped so hard he could hardly hear her. He didn't need to; he knew what she meant. Still... "Emily, I can't take advantage of you."

"I'm not asking you to. But hey, if you don't want to—"

"*Want* has nothing to do with it."

She leaned in close to him. "Actually, it has everything to do with it."

WED IN THE WEST:
New Mexico's the perfect place
to finally find true love!

Dear Reader,

Home is a concept I find myself exploring in all my stories, since home is so much more than simply an address. Because how and what we think of as home so often defines us as people, shaping our personalities, our ability to relate to our other humans and our outlook on life.

After major shake-ups in both their lives, Colin and Emily are forced to rethink what home means to them—Colin as he questions the pull back to his roots, and Emily as she discovers that she can't even define what home means to her until she comes to terms with who she really is. And both of them have some serious thinking to do about family, as well. As in, what it's always been...or what it could be going forward. On the surface, it's not exactly the best soil for love to grow...or is it?

I hope you enjoy watching the last of the four Talbot brothers find his perfect match as much as I loved helping him along the path to happily-ever-after.

Blessings,

Karen

Falling for the Rebound Bride

Karen Templeton

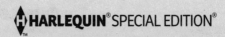
HARLEQUIN® SPECIAL EDITION®

Recycling programs
for this product may
not exist in your area.

ISBN-13: 978-0-373-62330-3

Falling for the Rebound Bride

Copyright © 2017 by Karen Templeton-Berger

Printed in U.S.A.

Karen Templeton is an inductee into the Romance Writers of America Hall of Fame. A three-time RITA® Award—winning author, she has written more than thirty novels for Harlequin. She lives in New Mexico with two hideously spoiled cats. She has raised five sons and lived to tell the tale, and she could not live without dark chocolate, mascara and Netflix.

Books by Karen Templeton

Harlequin Special Edition

Wed in the West

Back in the Saddle
A Soldier's Promise
Husband Under Construction
Adding Up to Marriage
Welcome Home, Cowboy
A Marriage-Minded Man
Reining in the Rancher
A Mother's Wish

Jersey Boys

Meant-to-Be Mom
Santa's Playbook
More Than She Expected
The Real Mr. Right

Summer Sisters

The Marriage Campaign
A Gift for All Seasons
The Doctor's Do-Over

The Fortunes of Texas: Whirlwind Romance

Fortune's Cinderella

Visit the Author Profile page
at Harlequin.com for more titles.

To my five guys
Who made our home
more than we could have ever imagined.
Love you.

Chapter One

The young woman had been eyeing him from the other side of the luggage carousel for several minutes, her pale forehead slightly crimped. Far too wiped out to be paranoid—or return her interest, if that's what it was—Colin instead focused on his phone as he reflexively massaged an unyielding knot in the back of his neck. Although truthfully his entire body was one giant screaming ache after nearly two days either on a plane or waiting for one—

"Um... Colin? Colin Talbot?"

Instinctively clutching his camera bag, he frowned into a pair of sweet, wary blue eyes he was pretty sure he'd never seen in his life. Clearly he was even more tired than he'd realized, letting her sneak up on him like that.

With a squeaky groan, the carousel lurched into action, the contents of the plane's belly tumbling down the chute, bags and boxes jostling each other like a bunch of sleepy drunks. The other passengers closed in, ready to pounce, many sporting the standard assortment of cowboy hats and beat-up boots you'd expect to see in New Mexico. Colin squinted toward the business end, keeping one grit-scraped eye out for his beat-up duffel, then faced the young woman again. Crap, his backpack felt like it weighed a hundred pounds. Not to mention his head.

"Have we met? Because I don't—"

"I was a kid, the last time I saw you," she said, a smile flicking across a mouth as glossy as her long, wavy hair, some undefined color between blond and brown. "When I visited the ranch." She tucked some of that shiny hair behind one ear, the move revealing a simple gold hoop, as well as lifting the hem of her creamy blouse just enough to hint at the shapely hips her fitted jeans weren't really hiding. Hell. Next to this perfect specimen of refinement, Colin felt like week-old roadkill. Probably smelled like it, too, judging from the way the dude next to him on that last leg from Dallas kept leaning away.

The smile flickered again, although he now saw it didn't quite connect with her eyes. She pressed a slender, perfectly manicured hand to her chest. "Emily Weber? Deanna's cousin?"

Deanna. His younger brother Josh's new wife. And their dad's old boss's daughter. Now, vaguely, Colin remembered the gangly little middle schooler who'd spent a few weeks on the Vista Encantada that summer more than ten years ago. Vaguely, because not only had he already been in college, but she was right, they hadn't talked much. If at all. Mostly because of the age difference thing. That she even recognized him now...

"Oh. Right." Colin dredged up a smile of sorts, before his forehead cramped again. "You don't look much like I remember."

Humor briefly flickered in her eyes. "Neither do you."

He shifted, easing the weight of the backpack. "Then how'd you know it was me?"

A faint blush swept over her cheeks. "I didn't, at first. Especially with the beard. But it's hard to ignore the tallest man in the room. Then I noticed the camera bag, and I remembered the photo I spotted at your folks' house, when I was there a few months ago for the wedding. Josh's wedding, I mean." She grinned. "There's been a few of those in your family of late."

Seriously, his brothers had been getting hitched like there'd been a "buy one, get two free" sale on marriage licenses. First Levi, then Josh—his twin younger brothers— and soon Zach, the oldest, would be marrying for the second time—

"In any case," she said, "enough pieces started fitting together that I decided to take a chance, see if it was you. Although you probably wondered who the creeper chick trying to pick you up was."

Colin glanced back toward the carousel. "Thought never crossed my mind."

Out of the corner of his eye, he caught her gaze lower to her glittery flat shoes. "Crazy, huh?" she said, looking up again. But not at him. "After all this time, both of us being on the same plane to Albuquerque."

"Yeah."

This time the sound that pushed from her chest held a definite note of exasperation. "I'm sorry, I didn't mean to intrude on your privacy or whatever. I just thought, since I did recognize you, it'd be weird not to say anything. Especially since we're probably both headed up to the ranch. Unless…" Another flush streaked across her cheeks. "You're not?"

Colin shut his eyes, as if that'd stop her words' pummeling. True, he was exhausted and starving and not at all in the mood for conversation, especially with some classy, chatty chick he barely remembered. A chatty chick who clearly didn't know from *awkward*. Or didn't care. But she was right, he was being an ass. For no other reason than he could. Cripes, his father would knock him clear into next week for that. Not to mention his mother.

"No. I am," he said, daring to meet her gaze. And the you've-gone-too-far-buster set to her mouth under it. A mouth that under other circumstances—although what those might be, God alone knew—might have even provoked a glimmer of sexual interest. Okay, more than a glimmer. But those days were long gone, stuffed in some bottom drawer of his brain where they couldn't get him in trouble anymore. "And I apologize. It was a rough flight. Part of it, anyway."

Although not nearly as rough as the weeks, months, preceding it.

Emily's gaze softened. Along with that damn mouth. Yeah, sympathy was the last thing he needed right now.

"From?"

Since his name was plastered all over the magazine spread along with the photos, it wasn't exactly a secret. "Serbia."

A moment of silence preceded, "And why do I get the feeling I should leave it there?"

His mouth tugged up on one side. "Because you're good at reading minds?"

She almost snorted, even as something like pain flashed across her features. "As if. Then again…" Her gaze slid to his, so impossible to read he wondered if he'd imagined the pain in it. "Perhaps some minds are easier to read than others?"

Nope, not taking the bait. Even if he'd had a clue what the bait was. His arms folded across a layer of denim more disreputable than his yet-to-appear duffel, he said, "You get on in DC? Or Dallas?"

"DC."

"And nobody's picking you up?"

Her mouth twisted. "It was kind of last-minute. So I told Dee I'd rent a car, save her or Josh the five-hour round trip. They've got their hands full enough with the kids and the ranch stuff this time of year, and I can find my own way." Her eyes swung to his again. "What about you?"

"They don't know I'm here."

That got a speculative look before she snapped to attention like a bird dog. "Oh, there's one of my bags—"

"Which one?"

"The charcoal metallic with the rose trim. And there's the two others. But you don't have to—"

"No problem," Colin said, lugging the three hard-sided bags off the belt. Gray with pink stripes. Fancy. And no doubt expensive. His gaze once more flicked over her outfit, her hair and nails, even as his nostrils flared at her light, floral perfume.

Rich girl whispered through his brain, as another memory or two shuffled along for the ride, that his new sister-in-law's mother had hailed from a socially prominent East Coast family, that there'd been murmurings about how Deanna's aunt hadn't been exactly thrilled when her only sister took up with a cowboy and moved to the New Mexico hinterlands. Something about her throwing her life away. A life that had ended far too soon, when Deanna had only been a teenager.

Not that any of this had anything to do with him. Didn't then, sure as hell didn't now. Never mind the knee-to-the-groin reaction to the charmed life this young woman had undoubtedly led. The sort of life that tended to leave its participants with high expectations and not a whole lot of understanding for those whose lives weren't nearly so privileged—

"Hey. You okay?"

Colin gave his head a sharp shake, refusing to believe he saw genuine concern in those blue eyes. Apparently the long trip had chewed up more than a few brain cells.

"I'm fine. Or will be," he said as he grabbed his bag off the belt, dumping its sorry, chewed-up self on the airport's floor beside the shiny trio. "Nothing a shower, some food and a real bed won't fix." Not to mention some sorely needed alone time. "And the sooner we get—" *home*, he'd started to say, startling himself "—back to the Vista, the sooner I can make that happen." Slinging the duffel over his shoulder with the camera bag and commandeering the smaller two of Emily's bags, he nodded toward the rental car desk across the floor. "So let's go get our cars and get out of here."

Jerking up the handle of the larger bag, Emily frowned. "Um…why rent two cars? Wouldn't it make more sense to share one? Besides, don't take this the wrong way, but you do not look like someone up for driving through a couple hundred miles of nothing. In the dark, especially. So I'll drive, how's that?"

That got a momentary sneer from the old male ego— because Old Skool Dude here, the man was supposed to drive—until weariness slammed into him like a twenty-foot tidal wave. And along with it *logic*, because the woman had a point. Didn't make a whole lot of sense to rent two separate vehicles when they were going to the same place.

Not to mention the fact that passing out and careening into a ravine somewhere wasn't high on his to-do list. However…

"You might not want to be confined with me in a closed

space for two-and-a-half hours." Her brows lifted. "I think I smell."

She laughed. "Not that I've noticed. But it's warm enough we can leave the windows open."

"Once we get up past Santa Fe? Doubtful. Spring doesn't really get going good until May, at least."

A shrug preceded, "So I'll put on another layer—"

"But what'll you do for a car once you're there?"

"Dee said there's a truck I can use, if I want. So I was gonna turn in the rental tomorrow in Taos, anyway…"

First off, that shrug? Made her hair shimmer around her shoulders, begging to be touched. So wrong. Second, the image of Emily's perfectly polished person collided in Colin's worn-to-nubs brain with whatever undoubtedly mud-caked 4x4 her cousin was referring to. The ranch vehicles weren't known for being pretty.

Unlike the woman with the shimmery hair who'd be driving one of them.

So wrong.

Then he dragged his head out of his butt long enough to catch the amused smile playing around her mouth. "You really have a problem sharing a ride with me?"

Colin's cheeks heated. "It's not you."

"Actually, I got that. No, really. But I'm beginning to understand what Josh said about you being a loner—"

"I'm not—"

"Even I know you haven't been home in years," she said gently. "That you've barely been in touch with anyone since you left. And then you don't even tell your family you're coming back? Dude. However," she said, heading toward the rental desk, her hair swishing against her back. Glimmering. Taunting. "My only goal right now is to get to the ranch." She glanced back over her shoulder at him, and once again he saw a flicker of something decidedly sharp edged. "Expediency, you know? Your issues are none of my business. Nor are mine yours. In fact, we don't even have to talk, if you don't want to. I won't be offended, I promise. So. Deal?"

With the devil, apparently.

"Deal," Colin grumbled, hauling the rest of the bags to the desk, wondering why her reasonableness was pissing him the hell off.

An hour later, Emily had to admit Colin had been right about two things: the farther north they went, the colder it got; and he was definitely a little on the gamey side. Meaning she'd had no choice but to keep the windows at least partly down, or risk suffocation.

Also, it was *dark*. As in, the headlight beams piercing the pitch blackness were creepy as all get-out. To her, *night* meant when the street lamps came on, not that moment when the sun dived behind the horizon and yanked every last vestige of daylight with it. Her heart punched against her ribs—so much for her oh-I'll-drive bravado back there in the airport, when for whatever reason it hadn't occurred to her she'd never actually driven the route before. Somebody had always ferried her to and from Albuquerque. Sure, she would've made the trek herself in any case, but being responsible for another human being in the car with her...

"Jeez, get a grip," she muttered, turning up the Sirius radio in the SUV, hoping the pulsing beat would pound her wayward thoughts into oblivion. Not to mention her regrets, crammed inside her head like the jumbled mess of old sweaters and jeans and tops she'd stuffed willy-nilly inside her pretty new luggage. Clothes that predated Michael, that she'd rarely worn around him because he'd said they made her look dumpy.

Emily's nostrils flared as her fingers tightened around the leather-padded wheel. Someday, she might even cry.

Someday. When she was over the hurling and cursing stage.

Beside her, a six-feet-and-change Colin snorted and shifted, his arms folded over his chest as he slept. They'd barely made it out of Albuquerque before he'd crashed, his obvious exhaustion rolling off him in waves even more than the funk. If it hadn't been for that picture Dee had shown Emily—a very serious publicity shot of Colin the photojournalist—she would've never recognized him. As it was, between the five days' beard growth and shaggy hair, the rumpled clothes and saddlebags under his eyes, she still wasn't sure how she had. It must've been the eyes, a weird pale green against his sun-weathered face—

Emily released another breath, aggravation swamping her once more. Although with herself more than Colin, she supposed, for not having the good sense to leave well enough alone. Gah, it was as though she'd been totally incapable of stanching the words spewing from her mouth. Apparently heart-slicing betrayal had that effect on her. But seriously—after a lifetime of making nice, *now* she couldn't resist poking the bear? And a grumpy, malodorous one at that?

From her purse, her phone warbled. Her mother's ringtone. Good thing she was currently driving, because… No.

The man shifted again, muttering in his sleep, the words unintelligible. She imagined a frown—since that seemed to be his face's default setting, anyway—

"Crap!"

At the laser-like flash of the animal's eyes, Emily swerved the car to the right, hard, the wheels jittering over rocks and weeds before jerking to a spine-rattling stop. Colin's palm slammed against the dash as he bellowed awake, a particularly choice swearword hanging in the cold air between them for what felt like an hour.

"What the hell?"

"S-something darted out in front of the c-car," Emily finally got out, over the sudden—and horrifying—realization of exactly how close she was to losing it.

"You okay?"

How a gruff voice could be so gentle, Emily had no idea. How she was going to keep it together in the face of that gentleness, she had even less of one. But she would. If it killed her.

Her neck hurt a little when she nodded. "I'm fine."

"You don't sound fine."

On a half-assed laugh, she leaned her head back. Or would have if the headrest had let her. "I almost took out Bambi. What do you think?" She dared to cut her eyes to his, only to realize she couldn't see them anyway. Thank goodness. "Sorry about the sudden stop. Is everything… Are you…?"

"I'm good. Or will be when my heart climbs back down out of my throat." Which he now cleared. "Good save, by the way."

"How would you know?" she said, even as pleasure flushed her cheeks. "Since you slept through it."

"We're still upright. And alive. So I count that as a win."

"Funny, you don't strike me as a look-on-the-bright-side type."

"You'd be surprised."

"I already am. Well." And her heart could stop break-dancing anytime now, she thought as she gripped the wheel. "I guess we should get going—"

"You're shaking."

"Only a little… What are you doing?"

This asked as he got out of the car and walked around

to her side, motioning for her to open the door. "Taking over the driving, what does it look like?"

"You don't have to—"

"Actually, I think I do."

Emily felt her face go grumpy. "I thought you said that was a good save."

"It was. And I mean that. But I'm awake now—"

"Sorry about that."

"—and I'm probably a little better at recovering from stress than you are."

"Heh. You ever driven on the DC beltway?"

"Many times. Although trust me, it doesn't even begin to compare with Mumbai. Besides, once we hit town, do you have any idea where we're going?"

There was that. Because, again, she hadn't driven when she'd been out before. Of course her plan had been to either rely on the car's GPS or—probably better—on Dee or Josh. Which she could still do. But by now she realized she was beginning to slip across that fine line between independent and mule-headed. And she was whacked, too.

"Emily?"

Again with the gentleness. Jerk.

"Fine," she said, climbing down from behind the wheel and marching around to the passenger side, huddling deeper into her sweater coat before strapping herself in. Rocks crunched and rattled as Colin pulled back onto the highway, and Emily felt her jangled nerves relax. A little.

Because for some reason this guy seemed a lot bigger awake than he had asleep. And she wasn't exactly tiny. A fact that had apparently induced no small amount of angst in her petite mother—

"So where are we, exactly?" Colin asked.

"Just past Taos."

He nodded. "You mind if I turn down the…music?"

"Turn it off, if you want. I don't care."

"You sure?"

"I'm sure."

Except the silence that followed made her brain hurt. Strange how she didn't mind the quiet when she was actually by herself. But when there was actually someone else in the space—

"So how come you didn't tell anyone you were coming?"

He hesitated, then said, "Because I didn't want to."

"None of my business, in other words."

His gaze veered to hers, then away.

"And you don't think they might find it weird when we show up together?"

A single-note chuckle pushed through his nose. "Dog with a bone, aren't cha?"

Her mouth pulled flat, Emily shoved her hair behind her ear. But after years of being the peacemaker, the One Most Likely to Back Down… "Guess I don't have a whole lot of patience these days for secrets."

"Even though this has nothing to do with you."

"Me, no. My cousin, yes. And her husband. And his family. So…"

"And you're nothing if not loyal."

She waited out the stab to her heart before saying, "Out of fashion though that might be."

That got a look. Probably accompanied by a frown, though she wasn't about to check.

Another couple miles passed before he said, "And I'm guessing I've been the topic of conversation recently."

"Your name does come up a lot," she said quietly, then glanced over. "Since, you know, you're the brother who's not there. And hasn't *been* there for years."

Seconds passed. "I've been…on assignment."

Exactly what Josh had said, after his and Dee's wedding, his that's-life shrug at complete odds with the disappointment in his eyes. And between the leftover shakiness from nearly taking out that deer back there and feeling like hornets had set up shop inside her brain, whatever filters Emily might have once had were blown to hell.

"From everything I can tell, Colin, your family's great. In fact, most people would be grateful..." Tears biting at her eyes, she gave her head a sharp shake, rattling the hornets. "So what exactly did they do to tick you off so much?"

And to think, Colin mused, if he hadn't agreed to this crazy woman's suggestion to share the car, the worst that might've happened would have been his ending up in a ditch somewhere.

Of course, he didn't owe her, or anyone, an explanation. Although she seemed like a nice enough kid—if pushy—and surprisingly playing the total bastard card wasn't part of his skill set. Besides, in a half hour they'd be there, and he'd hole up in one of the cabins, and she'd stay with her cousin in the main house, and they probably wouldn't even see each other again for the duration of her visit. Right?

Except right now she was watching him, waiting for an answer, those great, big, sad eyes pinned to the side of his face. Yeah, there was a story there, no doubt. Not that he was about to get sucked in. Because he'd come home to get his head on straight again, not get all snarled in someone else's.

"They didn't *do* anything, okay?" he finally mumbled. "Like you said, they're great people. It's just we don't see a lot of things through the same lens."

He sensed more than saw her frown before she leaned into the corner between the seat and the door—at least as much as the seat belt would let her—her arms folded over her stomach. Thinking, no doubt.

"So what's different now?"

"Do you even consider what's about to pop out of your mouth before it does?"

"Probably about as much as you've considered their reaction when you show up out of the blue. And with your dad's heart condition—"

"First off, people keeling over from shock only happens in the movies—"

"Not only in the movies."

"Mostly, then. And second, Dad's not at death's door. He never was, as far as I can tell—"

"And how would you know that if you haven't been there?"

"Because that's what he said, okay? For crying out loud, I did talk to him, or Mom, or both, every day at the time. I'm not totally out of the loop—"

"Even if you prefer to hover at its edge?"

If it hadn't been for the gentle humor in her voice—and something more, something he couldn't quite put his finger on—he would've been a lot more pissed than he was. "They told me not to come home, that it wasn't necessary. And my reasons for returning now…" He briefly faced her, then looked away. "Are mine."

"As are your reasons for not giving them a heads-up that you are. Got it."

"You're really aggravating, you know that?"

Her laugh startled him. "Then my work here is done," she said, clearly pleased with herself. Because the chick was downright bonkers. Story of his life, apparently.

"Look," he said, giving in or up or whatever. "If you've been around my family for more than thirty seconds you know they can be a mite…overwhelming en masse."

Another laugh. "I noticed."

"So if I'd called my brother and told him I was coming, you can bet your life the whole gang would be at the Vista to welcome me home." His jaw clenched. "Maybe even the whole town. I know what I'm about to face, believe me. But I'd at least prefer to ease back into the bosom of the clan on my own terms. At least as much as possible."

"I can understand that."

"Really?"

"Like you're the only person in the world who has issues with their family?" she said quietly, not looking at him. "Please."

The sign for Whispering Pines flashed in the headlights, and Colin turned off the highway onto the smaller road leading to the tiny town. Emily shrugged more deeply into her coat; the higher they climbed, the colder the night got. But the air was sweet and clear and clean. And, Colin had to admit, welcoming.

"It's the space, isn't it?" she said, shattering his thoughts.

"Excuse me?"

"Why you've come home. Same reason I'm here now, I suppose. To stop the—" She waved her hands at her head, then folded her arms again. "The noise. The crowding."

The impulse to probe nudged more insistently. He'd assumed she was only there to visit, like people did. Normal people, anyway. Or to attend Zach's wedding, although that wasn't for weeks yet. Now, though, questions niggled. Maybe there was more…?

And whatever that might be had nothing to do with him.

"Hadn't really thought about it," he muttered, ignoring what had to be a doubtful look in response. Shaking her head, Emily dug her phone out of her purse, only to heave a sigh and slug it back inside.

"No signal. Jeez, how do people even survive out here?"

"Same way they have for hundreds of years, I imagine."

A soft grunt was her only reply. Thank God. Although Colin had to admit, as wearying as her poking and prying had been, the silence was far worse, providing a far-too-fertile breeding ground for his own twisted-up thoughts. Because despite the universe's insistence that this is where he needed to be right now, he'd be lying to himself if he didn't admit this felt an awful lot like starting over.

Or worse, failure.

A dog's barking as they pulled into the Vista's circular driveway shattered the silence, although Colin barely heard it over his pounding heart, the rush of blood between his ears. Beside him, Emily gathered her giant purse, then gave him what he suspected was a pitying look before grabbing the door's handle.

"I don't envy you right now," she murmured, then shoved open the door and got out. By now her cousin and his brother were out on the oversize veranda. Even in the screwy light he could see confusion shudder across both their faces.

"You'll never guess who I ran into in the airport," she said, and Colin realized he had two choices: show himself, or turn right around and pretend this had all been a mistake. Except the flaw with plan B was that, for one thing, Emily's luggage was still in the SUV. And for another, she'd rat on him.

So, on a weighty sigh, Colin pried himself from behind the wheel and faced his little brother, who immediately spit out a cussword that would've gotten a good smack upside the head from their mother. Two seconds later, Josh was pounding the hell out of Colin's back, then grinning up at him like a damn fool.

"Holy hell, Col," he said, his eyes wet, and Colin did his best to grin back.

"I know, right?" he said, feeling heat flood his cheeks before he glanced over to see Emily wrapped tightly in his new sister-in-law's arms, bawling her eyes out.

Chapter Two

"So how come you didn't say anything?"

Standing at the sink in the ranch's ginormous, Southwest-kitsch kitchen, Emily set the now-clean Dutch oven in the drainer, pushing out a sigh for Colin's question. Not that she'd been able to eat much of the amazing pot roast, especially after embarrassing the hell out of herself earlier. But her cousin's keeping dinner warm for her—well, *them*, as it happened—had been a very sweet gesture. Because that was Dee.

Wiping her damp hands across her butt, Emily turned, now unable to avoid the scowl she'd ignored—more or less—all through the late dinner. Even from six or so feet away, Colin's size was impressive. At least he no longer looked—or smelled—as though he'd recently escaped from the jungle. And he'd shaved, which took the edge off the mountain man aura. Somewhat. But with his arms crossed over that impressive chest, not even his slightly curling, still-damp hair detracted from the massive mouth-drying solidity that was Colin Talbot. For sure, none of the brothers were exactly puny, but Colin was next door to intimidating. Toss in the glower, and...

Yeah.

"Your brother let you out of his clutches?"

The corner of Colin's mouth twitched. "For the moment. The dog was acting like something was going on outside he thought Josh needed to check out."

And Dee had gone to nurse her infant daughter—after Emily shooed her off, insisting on cleaning up after dinner. No buffers, in other words. And judging from that penetrating gaze, Colin was not-so-patiently waiting for her answer.

She shrugged, a lame attempt at playing it cool. "Maybe because your doing the prodigal son routine seemed like a far bigger deal than—"

"Your wedding getting called off?"

Weirdly, he sounded almost angry. Although whether it was because she hadn't told him, or on her behalf, she had no idea. Not that either of those made any sense. Then again, maybe he was ticked off because of a dozen other things she wasn't privy to. Nor was she likely to be. So Big Guy didn't exactly have a lot of room to talk, did he?

And before those weird, light eyes melted her brain, Emily turned back around to wipe down the sink. "In the interest of journalistic integrity," she said, scrubbing far harder than the stainless sink needed. "I was the one who called it off."

"Because your fiancé cheated on you. Josh filled me in."

The wrung-out sponge shoved behind the faucet, Emily faced him again, her arms tightly crossed over her ribs. "Seriously? You reconnect with your brother for the first time in a million years and you guys talk about *me*?"

"Hey. You were the one who totally lost it the minute we got here. Not me. Although for what it's worth, I didn't ask. Josh volunteered the information. And it was like a five-, six-second part of the conversation. Okay, ten at the most. But I thought you'd probably appreciate knowing that I know." He paused. "Not that I plan on being in your way much. In fact, I'm heading over to the foreman's cabin in a few."

Their gazes tangled for a long moment before Josh and the dog suddenly reappeared, the panting, grinning Aussie shepherd mix trotting over to his bowl to noisily slosh water all over the tiled floor.

"Have no idea what Thor heard," Josh said, striding to the sink to fill a glass of his own. Colin had a good three or four inches on his little brother, who still wasn't "little" by anyone's standards. The Talbots grew 'em solid, for sure. Josh's mossy eyes darted from her to Colin, a quizzical frown briefly biting into his forehead. But whatever he was thinking he kept to himself, thank goodness. Instead he flicked the empty glass toward the sink, then set it back in the drain board before clapping Josh's arm. "Well, come on—let's get you set up. Haven't been out there in weeks, have no idea what condition it's in—"

"Considering some of the places I've slept?" Colin said with a tight smile. "I'm sure it's fine. And I'm about to collapse. We can talk more tomorrow," he said gently at his brother's slightly let-down expression. "Although don't be surprised if I sleep until dinnertime. But promise me you won't tell Mom and Dad I'm here."

"I won't."

"Swear."

Chuckling, Josh pressed a hand to his heart. "To God. Good enough?"

With a nod, Colin walked to the back door where

he'd dumped his stuff; a moment later, he was gone, and Emily turned to her cousin-in-law. Squinting. Josh actually winced.

"Sorry, it kinda slipped out. Then again…" He leaned back against the counter, his palms curled over the edge. "It's not exactly a secret, is it?"

"No, but…" Emily glanced toward the door, where she could have sworn Colin's presence still shimmered. Which only proved he hadn't been the only wiped-out person in the house. "No," she repeated, giving Josh a little smile, which she transferred to the dog when he came over to nudge her hand with his sopping-wet snout. Then she sniffed, blinking back another round of tears.

"You know you can stay as long as you want," Josh said, adding, "I mean that," when Emily lifted watery eyes to his. "You probably have no idea how much Dee talked about you, when she came back after her dad died. About how you saved her sanity after that business with her ex. How you stood by her when your folks…well…"

At that, Emily pushed out a tiny laugh. "Yeah, propriety's kind of a biggie with them. Mom especially." Meaning a knocked-up niece hadn't been part of Margaret Weber's game plan. Although that was small potatoes compared with her daughter's society wedding getting the ax weeks before it was supposed to happen. Never mind that it would have been a total sham.

"In any case," Josh continued, "after everything you did for Dee, anything we can do to return the favor—"

"Thanks. But…"

Her cousin's husband grinned. "What?"

Emily sighed. In the rush of adrenaline that had followed in the wake of discovering Michael's secret, her fight-or-flight impulse had kicked in, big-time. And since fighting had felt like an exercise in futility, she'd chosen flight...as far from Michael and her mother and all those gasps and clacking tongues in McLean, Virginia, as she could get. And where else but to the place that had been a balm to her soul the few times she'd been here as a kid? And where the only person who could effortlessly toggle between being a nonjudgmental sounding board and understanding when Emily needed space lived?

However, now that the adrenaline was subsiding, it occurred to her that this was a newly married couple...a newly married couple with two young children between them, who probably cherished their alone time when said children were asleep. So the last thing they probably wanted, or needed, was some emotionally volatile chick invading their space.

"You guys have to promise me," she said to Josh's bemused expression, "you'll let me know the minute you feel I'm cramping your style."

At that, Josh laughed out loud. "We live with a four-year-old and an infant. Cramped *is* our style. As it will be for many years to come, I expect. Although at least *you* can get your own glass of water if you wake up in the middle of the night. You can, right?"

Emily chuckled. "Not only that, I can even make my own breakfast."

"Then there ya go." Josh leaned over to give her shoulder a quick squeeze. "In case you missed it, we're kinda big on family around here. So not another word, you hear?"

Her eyes burning again, Emily nodded. And this time, not because she was worn-out. Not even because of her own foolishness, letting herself get caught up in a fairy tale that now lay shattered in a million pieces at the bottom of her soul. That had been just plain stupid. Even so, she had no doubt she'd eventually recover. And be stronger for the experience, if not a whole lot wiser. So out of the ashes and all that.

But what yanked at her heart now was the sudden and profound realization of what had been missing from her life to this point, or at least not nearly as much in evidence as it should have been:

The good old Golden Rule, treating others the way you'd want to be treated. At least, as far as being on the receiving end of it went. All her life, it now occurred to her, she'd tried so hard to do what was expected of her, to not make waves. A lot in life she'd been fine with, for the most part. So sue her, she liked making people happy. But how often had anyone else ever done that for her? Other than Dee, that was, who'd come to live with Emily and her parents shortly after her mother died, when they were teenagers.

Now Emily looked at the kind, wonderful man her cousin had married, feeling overwhelmingly grateful for Deanna's happiness…and even more acutely aware of how badly she'd been screwed. And as her cousin joined them in the kitchen, one arm slipping around her husband's waist, resolve flooded Emily, that the next time—if there even was a next time—either the dude would look at her the way Josh looked at Dee or *fuggedaboutit*. Because God knew Michael had never looked at her like that, had he? And look how that had turned out.

"She asleep?" Josh asked Dee, who spiked a hand through her short dark hair. Almost chin length now, grown out from the edgier style she'd worn when she worked at that art gallery in DC. Roots were showing, too, a burnished glimmer against the black ends.

"Out like a light," Dee said, yawning as she leaned into Josh. Again, envy spiked through Emily, at how comfortable they were with each other. How much in love. Which was what came, Emily supposed, from their having been friends first, when they'd been kids and Josh's father had worked for Dee's. But between that and the trip and the events leading to the trip and the weirdness with Colin, Emily suddenly felt used up.

"If you guys don't mind," she said, "I think I'm going to turn in. It's been a long day."

"I'm sure," Dee said, slipping out of the shelter of her husband's embrace to wrap her arms around Emily, hold her close for a long moment. "We'll talk tomorrow. If you want."

"I'm sure I will," Emily said, then left the kitchen, letting the silence in the long, clay-tiled hall leading to the bedroom wing enfold her. Even with the updates to the house from when Dee and Josh thought they'd sell it after Uncle Granville's death, the place hadn't changed much from what she remembered from childhood. But the century-old hacienda, with its troweled walls and beamed ceilings, seemed good with that, like an old woman who saw no need to adopt the latest fashion craze simply because it was the latest thing.

A giant gray cat, curled on the folded-up quilt on the foot of the guest room's double bed, blinked sleepily at her when she turned on the nightstand's lamp. No one seemed to know how old Smoky was, or how he'd even come to live here—like a ghost whose presence was simply accepted.

"Hey, guy," she said, plopping her smaller bag onto the mattress, chuckling at his glower because she'd disturbed his nap. Not to mention his space, since he'd clearly staked a claim on the room in her absence. "We gonna be roomies for the next little while?"

The cat yawned, then meowed before hauling himself to his feet and plodding across the bed to bump her hand as she tugged a pair of pajamas from the case and zipped it back up. Unpacking would come later, a thought that hurt her chest. Not because she was here, but because of *why* she was here—

Dee's quiet knock on her open bedroom door made Emily start. Her cousin had changed into a loose camisole top, a pair of don't-give-a-damn drawstring bottoms and a baggy plaid robe that definitely gave off a masculine vibe.

"Need anything?"

"A new life?"

With a snort, her cousin came over to sit on the edge of the bed, which the cat took as an invitation to commandeer her lap. "I know I said tomorrow," she said as Emily unceremoniously disrobed, tugged on the pajamas. Unlike her relationships with nearly everybody else in her life, she and Dee had no secrets between them. "But... I'm so sorry, Em."

Emily crawled up onto the bed, sitting cross-legged to face Dee like she used to when they were kids. The cat immediately changed loyalties, flicking his poofy tail across Emily's chin before settling in, rumbling like a dishwasher. Smiling, she stroked his staticky fur.

"Better now than later, right?"

Her cousin blew a half laugh through her nose. "At least you're not pregnant," she muttered, then frowned. "You're not, are you?"

It was everything Emily could do not to laugh herself at the absurdity of her cousin's perfectly reasonable question. Especially since the sweet baby girl down the hall wasn't Josh's, but the result of Dee's affair—well before she moved back to New Mexico and reconnected with Josh, whom she hadn't seen since she was a teenager— with a man who'd neglected to mention he already had three children. And a wife. A thought that immediately displaced Emily's inappropriate spike of amusement with anger, at how both she and her cousin had been played for fools by a pair of scumbags who mistook agreeableness for weakness.

Or stupidity.

"What do you think?" she said, and her cousin's mouth twisted.

"Oh. Right. Although sometimes—"

"Not in this case. Although I suppose I should see about having the IUD removed now. Since…" She shrugged, and Dee's eyes went soft.

"Since it's completely over between you and Michael?"

"Yeah," Emily said on a sigh.

"Well…" Dee grinned. "Before you do, who's to say you couldn't have some good old-fashioned revenge sex?"

Now Emily did laugh. Ridiculous though the suggestion was. Towns this small weren't exactly rife with prospects. Which right now was a major selling point, actually, what with her recent self-diagnosis of acute testosterone intolerance. "With…?"

Her cousin's eyes twinkled. "I'm sure we can scrounge up someone who isn't toothless and/or on Social Security."

"Meaning Colin," Emily deadpanned, and Dee's eyebrows nearly flew off her head.

"The thought never even entered my head."

"Right."

"You've gotta admit, he does clean up nice." Emily glared. For many reasons. Then her cousin leaned forward to wrap her hand around hers. "You do know I'm kidding, right?"

"I'm never sure with you."

"Good point," Dee said, the twinkle once again flashing. "But while I do find it serendipitous—"

"Ooh, big word."

"—that the two of you showed up together, and he is a hunk—because clearly the Talbots don't know how to make 'em any other way—it's also pretty obvious he's no more in the market for fun and games than you are."

"Yeah, I kind of got that impression, too. But what did he say? To Josh?"

"It's more what he didn't say, I think. Obviously the man is all about keeping to himself. Even more than most men are," she said, and Emily thought, *Tell me about it*. "But he indicated to Josh he just needed a break. And that it'd been too long since he'd been home. Especially since so much has happened since then. Weddings and whatnot."

"You think he'll stick around for Zach and Mallory's?"

"Who knows? I get the feeling Colin's not big on plans. Or commitments." Dee cocked her head. "And what's with that look?"

Emily punched out a sound that was equal parts laugh and sigh. "That would be me overthinking things I have no business thinking about at all. Especially since I clearly have no talent whatsoever when it comes to guessing what's going on inside someone's head. I mean, really—I knew Michael for *how* many years? And still..." She shook her head. "So presuming anything about some man I've known for a few hours—and half of that he's either been comatose or not around..."

"Em." Dee looked almost exasperated. "First off, there's a huge difference between some dirtwad who's deliberately trying to keep you in the dark and a guy who's simply not big on sharing. With anybody, apparently. Even his brothers barely know him, for reasons known only to Colin. So if you think Colin's got some serious issues—believe me, you're not alone. In fact, Josh said the same thing. Only *I* think—" she squeezed Emily's hand "—that you've got enough junk of your own to work through right now without worrying about someone you don't even know. Because secondly, you're too damn kindhearted. Always have been. Which is probably…" She bit her lip, and Emily rolled her eyes.

"Go on, spit it out. Which is why I'm in this mess, right?"

"Seeing the best in people is what you do," Dee said gently. "Who you are. And I wouldn't change that, or you, for the world. So don't even go there, you hear me? But it does have its downside."

"In other words I need to toughen up."

"Says the woman who teaches kindergartners," Dee said on a short laugh. "You're plenty tough, babycakes. But I think…" Her cousin paused, her eyes narrowed slightly. "What's the longest you've ever gone without a boyfriend? A month? Two?"

Emily started. "I…I don't know. I never really thought about it—"

"Because you've never been alone long enough *to* think about it. And then you reconnected with Michael at that thing at the club, and everyone—his parents, your parents—were all *ooh, perfect*, and…"

"And I fell right into everyone's expectations."

Her cousin's smile was kind. "Especially Aunt Margaret's."

Considering her mother's apoplectic fit when the wedding was called off? Truth. But…

"You never really liked Michael, did you?"

Dee reached over to stroke the cat. "I never really *trusted* him. Gut reaction, sorry. But at first I figured it would probably peter out, so why say anything? Especially since nobody made me God. Then you guys got engaged, and… I don't know. Something felt off. Except then *I* got involved with Phillippe, and, well. Considering how that turned out, I didn't exactly have room to talk, did I? And by then you were deep into wedding-planning fever..." She shrugged, then gave her cousin a little smile.

"You could've still said something."

Her cousin snorted. "And would you have listened? Or taken my 'feelings' as sour grapes because my own relationship had ended so badly? In fact," she said before Emily could answer, "I wasn't all that sure myself I could be objective. Because at that point I pretty much hated anything with a penis."

Clapping a hand to her mouth, Emily unsuccessfully smothered her guffaw. Then she lowered it, still chuckling, only to release another breath. "I can relate, believe me."

"Seriously."

Emily's eyes burned. "You know what's really sad? At this point I don't even know if I was really happy—before the truth came out—or just thought I was."

"Sing it, honey," Dee sighed. "But the good news is, at least we grow. Our hearts get shattered and then we get mad and then we get to work. Which doesn't in the least absolve the creeps of their creepiness. But we gain so much more from the experience than we lose."

"How...adult of you."

"I know, right?" Grinning, Dee levered herself off the bed, tugging her robe closed in the desert chill. "You're gonna be fine, Em. You *are* fine. And you know what else?"

"What?"

Her cousin's gaze softened again. "You're free," she said, bending over to kiss Emily's hair before padding out of the room.

For several seconds after, Emily sat on the bed, stroking the cat who'd returned to smash himself up beside her, his purr comforting and warm.

You're free...

Her eyes watered as the words played over and over in her head. Because for the first time that she could remember...she was, wasn't she? Free from anyone else's *expectations*, like Dee said. Or judgment, or censure. Free *to* finally figure out who she was, what *she* wanted.

More to the point, what she didn't.

True, she'd come for the space. Absolutely. But not to escape. Instead, for the space to claim for herself everything that was rightfully hers.

Including, she realized, the luxury of being herself.

Of being able to do exactly as she pleased without worrying, or even caring, about what anybody else thought.

The headiness almost made her dizzy.

The next morning, Colin sat outside his parents' little house in town, trying to get his bearings before facing them. It didn't help that, despite his exhaustion—or maybe because of it—he hadn't slept worth spit the night before. Didn't help that Emily kept popping into his head, although he assumed that was because she reminded him a touch of Sarah. A touch. The long hair, maybe. Her... freshness. That guileless, direct gaze that revealed more than she probably realized.

More than he could possibly handle. Especially after Sarah.

Especially now.

Releasing a breath, Colin got out of the rental and headed toward the house, shrugging into a denim jacket older than God as he sidestepped the same dinged pickup his mom had been driving for years. The impossibly blue sky framed the small brown house, squat and unassuming behind the huge lilac bushes beginning to leaf out beside the front door, the half dozen whiskey barrels choked with mounds of shivering pansies.

Despite the chill, Colin stopped for a moment, taking in the view. The house sat on the apex of a shallow cul-de-sac in a chorus line of a dozen others similar in size, if not in shape or color. There'd been no plan to Whispering Pines, it'd just sort of happened, lot by lot, house by house. But scraping the outskirts of town the way it was, this lot at least had a decent view of the mountains, which probably made Dad happy. It'd been damn good of Granville to give them the house, after the doctors *strongly* suggested Dad retire. There'd been other provisions, as well. His parents would never starve or be homeless. Still, three generations of Talbots had grown up in the ranch foreman's house, and it'd felt strange sleeping there—or trying to—last night by himself.

It felt strange, period, being here. Even though—

He jolted when the front door opened, although not nearly as much as his mother when she realized who was standing in her driveway. Her hair was more silver than he remembered, the ends of her long ponytail teasing her sweatered upper arms poking out from a puffy, bright purple vest. But her unlined face still glowed, her jeans still hugged a figure as toned as ever and the joy in those deep brown eyes both warmed him and made him feel like a giant turd. It wasn't that he didn't love his family, but—

"Holy crap," she breathed, appropriately enough, and Colin felt a sheepish grin steal across his cheeks.

"Hey, Mom," he said, and a moment later she'd thrown her arms around him—as much as she could, anyway, he had a good eight or nine inches on her—and was hugging and rocking him like he was three or something, the whole time keening in his ear. Then Billie Talbot held him apart and bellowed, "Sam! Get your butt out here, now!" and a minute later his father appeared, his smile even bigger than his wife's. Then Dad practically shoved Mom aside to yank Colin into a hug that almost hurt.

"Don't know why you're here," Dad mumbled, "don't care. Just glad you are."

Feeling his chest ease—because honestly, he'd had no idea how this was going to go down—Colin pulled away, shoving his hands in his back pockets. He'd always thought of his father as this giant of a man, towering over most everybody. Especially his sons. Now Colin realized he was actually a little taller than Sam, which somehow didn't feel right.

"Me, too." He paused. "It's been too long."

"Won't argue with you there," Dad said. Although despite that whole it-doesn't-matter spiel, Dad was no one's fool. Especially when it came to his sons, all of whom had pulled their fair share of crap growing up. And now it was obvious from the slight tilt of his father's heavy gray brows that he knew damn well there was more to Colin's return than a simple "it was time."

"So, where are you staying?" Mom asked. Colin faced her, now noticing she had her equipment bag with her, meaning she was headed out either to a birth or at least an appointment.

"In your old digs," he said with a slight smile.

"So you've seen Josh and them?"

He nodded. "But they didn't know I was coming, either. Neither did anyone else. Zach or Levi, I mean. I'm…easing back into things."

His mother got a better grip on the bag, then dug her car keys out of her vest's pocket. "And unfortunately it's my day at the clinic, so I can't hang around. But dinner later, yes?"

Colin smiled. "You bet."

Mom squeezed his arm, then said, "Oh, to hell with it," before pulling him in for another hug. This time, when she let go, he saw tears. "You have just made my day, honey. Shoot, year. I can't wait until tonight."

"Me, too," Colin said, then watched as she strode out to her truck with the same purposeful gait as always. Nothing scared that woman, he thought. Nothing that he was aware of, anyway.

"She's busier than ever," Dad said behind him, making him turn. "Happier, too."

His twin brothers had been in middle school when Mom announced it was time she lived her own life, that she'd decided to become a midwife. And if for a while they'd all been like a pile of puppies whose mama had decided they needed weaning, right then and there, they'd all gotten over it, hadn't they?

"Um…want something to drink?" Dad said, scrubbing his palm over the backside of his baggy jeans—an uncharacteristically nervous gesture, Colin thought. Mom'd said his father had lost weight after that scare with his heart, even if only because the doctors had put the fear of God in him. Apparently, however, it hadn't yet occurred to him to buy clothes to fit his new body. "It's probably too early for a beer, and I only have that 'lite' crap, anyway…"

Colin chuckled, even as he realized his own heart was stuttering a bit, too. True, he'd never butted heads with his father like his brother Levi had, but neither was there any denying that the day he'd left Whispering Pines for college he'd felt like a caged bird finally being set free. Nor had he ever expected any desire to come home to roost.

"That's okay, I'm good."

Nodding, his dad tugged open the door, standing aside so Colin could enter. The place was tiny, but as colorful and warm as the old cabin had been. Plants crowded windowsills with wild exuberance, while hand-quilted pillows and throws in a riot of colors fought for space on otherwise drab, utilitarian furniture. Interior design had never been part of Mom's skill set—and certainly not Dad's, whose only criteria for furnishings had been a chair big enough to hold him and a table to eat at—but there was love in every item in the room, from the lushness of her plants to how deliberately she displayed every item ever gifted to her from grateful clients.

Love that now embraced him, welcoming him home… even as it chastised him for staying away so long. But…

Colin frowned. "I would've thought if Granville was going to leave the ranch to a Talbot, it would've been to you."

His father snorted. "First off, I wouldn't've wanted it. Not at this point in my life. Which Gran knew. Second…" Dad's mouth twitched. "He also knew exactly what he was doing, leaving it to your brother and his daughter equally."

"Ah."

"Exactly. Because sometimes fate needs a little kick in the butt." Dad squinted. "So. What's going on, son?"

Underneath his father's obvious—and understandable—concern, Colin could still hear hints of the my-way-or-the-highway gruffness that'd raised his hackles a million times ever since he was old enough to realize there was a whole world outside of this tiny speck of it wedged beside a northern New Mexican mountain range. A world that needed him maybe, even if it'd be years before Colin figured out how, exactly. That hadn't changed, even if…

And the problem with voluntarily reinserting yourself

into the circle of the people who—for good or ill—loved you most was that there would be questions.

How truthfully Colin could answer those questions was something else again.

Chapter Three

Sucking in a slow, steady breath, Colin managed a smile. "Why am I back, you mean?"

Dad crossed his arms over what was left of his belly. But the fire in those fierce gray eyes hadn't diminished one bit. "Seems as good a place as any to start. Especially since your mother and me, we'd pretty much given up on that ever happening, to be truthful."

"I stayed in touch," Colin said, realizing how pitiful that sounded even before the words were out of his mouth.

"When it suited you, sure."

Even after all this time he still couldn't put into words what exactly had driven him away. Which was nuts. But all he'd known was that if he'd stayed he would've gone mad.

"I had things to do I couldn't do here," he said simply.

After a moment, his father started toward the nondescript but reasonably updated kitchen to pour himself a cup of coffee from the old-school Mr. Coffee on the counter. "Decaf," Dad groused, holding up the cup before taking a swallow and making a face. Then, leaning one roughened hand against the counter, he sighed. "Not gonna lie, for a long time it hurt like hell, after you left. That, on top of the crap Levi pulled…"

This said with an indulgent smile. Most likely because from everything Josh had said last night, his twin, Levi—who after a stint in the army was now back and married to the local girl he'd been secretly sweet on in school—and Dad had worked out their differences.

His father's gaze met his again. "Although I honestly don't know why I ever thought the four of you would stick around. That you'd naturally be as tied to the place as I was, and my daddy and granddaddy before me. No, let me finish, I've been waiting a long time to say this." Frowning, he glanced toward the window over the sink, then back at Colin. "Then this happened—" he gestured with the cup toward his chest "—and I guess when they put that stent in my artery more blood went to my brain and opened that up, too. And I realized if you expect your kids to be clones of you, you're not raising 'em right. You all have to follow your own paths, not mine. And I'm good with that." One side of his mouth lifted. "Mostly, anyway. But you can't blame me for being curious about what's prompted the surprise visit."

With that, it occurred to Colin his father hadn't seemed all that *surprised*, really. So much for swearing to God. "Josh told you I was here."

"He felt a heads-up wouldn't be a bad idea. I didn't tell your mother, though." His father chuckled. "After all these years—and raising you boys—it takes a lot to pull one over on her. Couldn't resist the opportunity to see the look on her face when you showed up. Although she will *kill* me if she ever found out I knew before she did."

Somehow, Colin doubted that. Sure, his folks bickered from time to time, same as any couple who'd been married a million years. They were human, after all. But there'd never been any doubt that Sam Talbot still, after those million years, knew he'd struck gold with Billie, who'd known a good thing—or so the story went—the instant she'd clapped eyes on the tall, lanky cowboy when she'd been barely out of school herself, and wouldn't do anything to jeopardize what they had. Even if she didn't let him get away with bubkes. It was all about balance with his mother, for sure.

Something Colin would do well to figure out for himself. And *by* himself.

Leaning against a pantry cupboard, he crossed his arms. "I got offered a book contract from a big publisher, for a collection of my photo-essays over the past several years."

His father's brows shot up. "Really?"

Colin nodded. "But I want to add some new material, too. So I need…" His mouth set, he glanced away, then back at his father. "I need someplace quiet to work. To sift through my thoughts about the subject matter."

"Which is?"

He felt his chest knot. "The plight of kids around the world."

Something flashed in his father's eyes. Colin couldn't tell—and didn't want to know, frankly—what. "Refugees, you mean?"

"Among others. Children living in poverty, in war-torn countries, whatever. I want…" He swallowed. "The whole reason I take pictures is so other people can see what I've seen."

"Sounds like quite an honor. That offer, I mean."

"I don't… That's not how it feels to me. It's more that—"

"It's your calling."

"I guess. A calling that came to me, though. I didn't go looking for it."

A smile barely curved his father's mouth. "That's how callings work, boy. They tend to clobber a person over the head. But your own place wouldn't work?"

"College kids in the next unit," Colin said, hoping his face didn't give him away. Although he wasn't lying. Exactly. "One thing they're not, is quiet."

His father's eyes narrowed, as though not quite buying the story. Hardly a surprise, considering he'd survived four teenage boys. Then his lips tilted again.

"And you know what? I'm not about to look a gift horse in the mouth. Or question its motives. I'm just glad you're here. For however long that turns out to be. And I cannot tell you how proud I am of you."

Holy hell—he couldn't remember his father ever saying that to him. About anything. Oh, Dad would occasionally nod appreciatively over something one or the other of them had done when they were kids, but actually giving voice to whatever he'd been thinking? Nope.

Old man hadn't been kidding about the blood flow thing.

"Thank you," Colin said.

And there was the nod. Because clearly Sam Talbot was as surprised as his son. Then he took another sip of his coffee, his brows drawn. "Josh also said Deanna's cousin Emily showed up with you."

Colin smiled. "I think it's more that I showed up with her. We were on the same flight coming in from Dallas."

"Pretty little thing."

"She is." Although not so little, actually. And of course now that Dad had brought her up, those mad, sad, conflicted eyes flashed in his mind's eye. No wonder, now that he knew the reason behind the ambivalence. In some ways it was probably worse for her, since she was younger. Fewer life experiences and all that—

"Well. Just wanted to touch base," Colin said, pushing away from the counter. For a moment disappointment flickered in his father's eyes—a previously unseen glimpse of a soft spot that rattled Colin more than he'd expected. Or was about to let on. "I need to get in some supplies before I can start work," he said gently. "But I'll be back for dinner, remember? Or we can go out, if you'd rather. My treat."

The right thing to say, apparently, judging from the way Dad perked right up. "That'd be real nice, either way. Depends on what your mother wants to do, of course."

"Of course. I'll call around five, see what's up."

They were back outside by now, where that chilly spring breeze grabbed at Colin's hair, slapped at his clean-shaven face. Patches of old snow littered the parts of the yard that didn't get direct sunlight, reminders that up this far, winter wasn't over until it said so…images that at one time would've been nothing more than benign reminders of his childhood. Now, not even the bright sunlight could mitigate other reminders, other images, of how cruel—for too many people—winter could be when *home* had been ripped out from under you.

"Sounds good," Dad said, palming the spot between Colin's shoulder blades. "When you planning on seeing your other brothers? Zach, especially—you two were so close as kids."

Colin supposed they had been, although age and isolation—and being roommates—had probably had more to do with that than temperament. Zach had been the quiet one, the steady one…the obedient one. The one Colin could count on to not judge when he'd go off about not being able to *wait* to get out of Whispering Pines.

"Maybe tomorrow," he said. "After I get settled." Although he supposed the sooner he got the reunion stuff out of the way, the sooner he could retreat into his work.

In theory, anyway.

Back in the rental car, Colin waved to his father as he pulled out of the driveway, then headed toward the only decent grocery store in town. He wished he could say he was looking forward to dinner that night. Except the problem with being around people who knew you—or thought they did, anyway—was the way things you didn't want leaked tended to leak out. He'd put his parents though enough as it was, even if he honestly couldn't say what he could've done differently while still being true to who he was. But for sure he wasn't about to dump on them now, or give them any reason to doubt he'd made the right choices. If nothing else, he owed them at least a little peace of mind, assurances that he was okay.

And if he wasn't…well, he'd figure it out. You know, like a grown man.

The store—all three aisles of it, more like some dinky Manhattan bodega than one of those mega suburban monstrosities—was mercifully empty on this weekday morning. And surprisingly well stocked with a bunch of chichi crap Colin had little use for. He could cook, after a fashion—at least, he'd moved beyond opening cans of soup and microwaving frozen burritos—but he was definitely about whatever took twenty minutes or less from package to stomach. Give him a cast-iron pan, a couple of pots, he was good.

He was about to toss a couple of decent-looking steaks into his cart when he heard, from the next aisle over, the women's laughter…the same laughter he'd heard at the dinner table the night before. Same as then, it wasn't so much the pitch of the laughs that set Deanna and her cousin apart as it was…the genuineness of them, he supposed. As in, one was actually happy, and the other was pretty much faking it. Although whether for her own sake or her cousin's, Colin had no idea.

Nor was it any of his concern.

They were talking about nothing of any real importance that he could tell. Not that he should be listening, but if they'd wanted privacy, yakking in a small store wasn't the best way to go about that. He plunked the steaks in the cart, worked his way over to the pork chops. Yep, he could still hear the two of them. Because again, small store. What he found interesting, though—from a purely analytic standpoint—was how different the cousins' voices were. Deanna's voice was lighter, sparklier, whereas Emily's was...

With a package of chicken legs suspended in his hand over the case, Colin paused, frowning as he caught another whiff of Emily's voice, and every nerve cell, from the top of his head to places that really needed to shut the hell up already, whispered, *Oh, yeah...*

Then he blinked, the fog dispersed and there she was. "Oh. Hi."

One thing about grocery store lights, they weren't known for being flattering. Meaning he probably looked like a neglected cadaver right now. And yet even without makeup—none that he could see, anyway—in a plain old black sweater and pair of jeans, her hair pulled back in a don't-give-a-damn ponytail, Emily was...okay, not *beautiful.* But definitely appealing.

Especially to a guy who hadn't had any in a while. And who, up to this very moment, had been perfectly fine with that. Or at least reconciled to it. Not liking at all where his thoughts—let alone his blood—were headed, Colin looked back at the chicken in his hand. "Hey," he said, realizing he looked about as dumb as a person could look. He finally tossed the chicken in the cart, then looked back at Emily.

Because what else was he supposed to do? Unfortunately, she still looked good. Especially with that amused smile.

"I'm, uh…" He waved at the half-filled cart. "Stocking up."

"Us, too. I promised I'd cook while I was here. In exchange for…" She flushed slightly. "It just seemed fair, that's all. Especially since Josh has his hands full with ranch stuff this time of year, and Dee's getting her gallery set up in town."

"Her gallery?"

"That's what she did, before she moved back. Worked at a gallery. Doing acquisitions and such. But this one will be all hers, showcasing local artists, she said. I figured I could at least help out while I was here. Instead of playing the guest."

Colin nodded. "You know how long you're gonna be here?"

"I'm…playing it by ear."

"You don't have a job or something to get back to?"

"No, actually. Not at the moment. I mean, I did, until…" Looking away, she rubbed her nose, then poked through the packages of ribs. "These are really good done in the Crock-Pot."

"That so?"

"You should look online, there are tons of recipes." By now not even the sucky florescent lighting could wipe out her blush, which started at her neckline and spread to her eyes, making him think of other kinds of flushes, which in turn made him seriously consider sticking his head in the nearest freezer case. "Well. I'll leave you to it. See you around?"

"Sure." *Oh, hell, no.*

Clutching her package of ribs, she walked away, her very pretty butt twitching underneath a layer of clingy denim, her hair all shiny and bouncy underneath the lights.

Colin would've groaned, but that would've been pathetic and juvenile.

But far worse than the kick to the groin was the tug at something a bit farther north, where empathy had staked a claim all those years ago. Because he could—and would—ignore the butt and the hair and, okay, the breasts pushing against the sweater. But those eyes…

Damn it. A blessing and a curse, both, being able to sense another's pain.

Especially when combined with the helplessness of knowing there wasn't a single damn thing you could do to alleviate it.

So. New goal, he thought as he pushed the cart up to the cashier, relieved to see the two women had apparently already checked out. Stay out of Emily Weber's way as much as possible while she was still here.

Which, with any luck, wouldn't be very long.

Limbo.

That was the only way to describe her current state of mind. Or current state, period, Emily thought as, breathing hard, she completed the loop around the ranch she'd been running every day for the past week. Oh, she'd been keeping busy for sure, cooking and cleaning and playing with little Austin and baby Katie, who was teething and drooly and fussy and absolutely adorable when she wasn't screaming her head off. And at least—she rounded the training corral between the main house and the old foreman's cabin—the stress and heartache were easing up… some. Although why she'd thought a week or two away would heal her, let alone really fix anything, she had no idea. At some point she'd have to return to real life, face her parents and her friends and everything she couldn't face before. As it was, she was ignoring her mother's calls, which had become more frequent *because* Emily was ignoring them. Although unfortunately she hadn't yet found the cojones to delete Mom's messages without listening to them.

Then again, maybe listening to them was proof she had more balls than she was giving herself credit for—

"Oh!"

Her cry wasn't enough to scare off the coyote, although the thing did glance her way, as if to ascertain whether Emily was worth its consideration. The critters weren't really much of a threat to the horses, apparently—at least, Josh only shrugged when she'd told him she'd also spotted one on her last run—but City Girl Emily still felt it wise to steer clear.

Until she noticed something fuzzy and small in the dirt about ten feet from the coyote. A possum? Squirrel? She couldn't tell. But the gray varmint, who'd clearly decided to ignore Emily, was closing in, and—

"Get out of here!" she yelled, flapping her arms like a madwoman and running toward the whatever-it-was, startling a bunch of birds from the top of the nearest piñon and spooking a trio of horses in the nearby pasture. "Go on! Get!"

The coyote hesitated, giving her a what-the-hell? look.

"I said—" Emily snatched a fair-sized stone off the ground and hurled it with all her might at the animal, where it pinged harmlessly in the dirt three feet in front of it, raising a cloud of dust. *"Get!"*

And damned if a spurt of pride didn't zing through her when the thing actually took off, loping up the road without looking back. Her heart hammering in her chest, Emily approached the small, now whimpering animal, her chest fisting when she realized it was a puppy. What kind and how old, she had no idea. And what to do next, she had even less. But she had to do something. Unfortunately, Dee and Josh were running errands separately with the kids, and while she knew Josh's brother Zach had his veterinary practice in town, she had no idea whether he was there or not. Besides which, her cousin and her husband had taken both trucks—

The puppy released the most heart-wrenching, plaintive cry ever, and Emily sank cross-legged onto the dirt to pull him into her lap, which was when she noticed dried blood on one of his paws. She carefully touched the spot and the poor little thing cried out in obvious pain. Damn. Hauling in a breath, Emily glanced over at the foreman's cabin a hundred or so yards away. The rental car was there, meaning Colin was probably home, but...

She gingerly hugged the mewling baby dog to her chest, stroking his soft fur and making soothing, if probably unhelpful noises. Despite Colin's living within spitting distance of the main house, they hadn't seen each other since that silly encounter in the grocery store. Dude had serious hermit tendencies, apparently. Although truth be told, given her reaction to him back there in the meat department Emily had been just as glad. Not because of the silly, awkward part, but definitely because of the dry-mouthed, wanting-to-plaster-herself-against-him part. Which flew in the face of everything she was. Or thought she was, anyway. As in, logical. Levelheaded. Not given to fits of insanity.

Never mind that simply sitting here thinking about Colin's mouth and jaw and eyes, *ohmigod*, and that little hollow at the base of his neck was making her feel as though molten ore was flowing through her veins.

"Jeez, girl," she muttered. "Get over it."

As if it was that easy. Because despite keeping busy, and running her butt off every day, and her determination to not think about her shattered heart and the bozo who'd shattered it, her heart had other ideas. In fact, the longer she was away, the more hurt and angry she got that she'd been played for a fool. That she'd let herself be played for a fool, taking the path of least resistance because…why? Because everyone else had been happy?

Clearly, she needed to majorly overhaul her definition of that word. Not to mention her expectations, she thought as her mouth twisted. Meaning she knew full well all this fizzing and bubbling was nothing more than a knee-jerk reaction to Michael's betrayal, a primitive—and completely ludicrous—urge to get even.

The pup whimpered again, nuzzling her collarbone…

Telling her wayward loins to shut the hell up, Emily heaved herself to her feet, the puppy cradled against her chest, and marched toward the cabin.

She thought maybe this was called taking back the reins.

Colin nearly jumped out of his skin when he caught Emily standing outside the front window with something furry clutched in one hand, waving like crazy at him with the other. And apparently yelling. Ripping out his earbuds, he set aside his laptop and reluctantly pushed himself off the leather couch, not even bothering to adjust his expression before opening the door. It'd taken two days before the right words had finally started to settle in his brain to accompany this particular photo. And now they were gone. So, yeah. Pissed.

Emily's flinch—and blush—should've given him more satisfaction than it did. Instead he felt like a jackass. For about two seconds, anyway, before all the reasons he'd gone out of his way to avoid her this past week came sailing back into his befogged brain. Because of that blush, for one thing. That her running togs left little to the imagination, for another. Toss in exercise glow and whatever the hell that scent was that she wore, the one that marched right in and rendered him an insentient blob of randy hormones, and—

His eyes dipped to the puppy, looking about as blissful as Colin imagined he would be cuddled against those breasts.

"Some coyote was trying to get him, or at least that's what it looked like, and I think he might be hurt but I don't have any way of getting him to the vet. If your brother's even at the clinic."

Colin dragged his gaze away from the pup—and her breasts—and to her eyes, a move which jarred loose his libido's stranglehold long enough for *Oh, hell,* to play through his brain.

"Let me see," he said, his knuckles grazing those breasts—damn—before he took the dog from her and carried him into the house. Emily followed, shutting the door behind her and sitting across from Colin when he sat back on the couch.

"Heaven knows how he got here—"

"Dumped, probably. It happens," he said to her stunned expression, then tenderly examined the bloodied paw. The pup whimpered again.

"Don't think it's broken, but I'm not the vet." He paused, gaze fixed on the dog and not on those worried blue eyes. Clearly his afternoon was shot. Not to mention his resolve. "I had dinner with Zach and them the other night, he said he's in the office every afternoon, all day on Saturdays, so…" Still holding the pup, he got to his feet. "So let's go get this little guy fixed up."

"Oh! Um…" Emily stood as well, rubbing her hands across her dusty bottom. Colin looked away. "If you'd lend me the car, I could take him, you don't have to come. I mean—" There went the pink cheeks again. "It's pretty obvious I interrupted you. I'm sure you want to get back to work."

She had. And he did. However…

"You know where the clinic is?"

"In…town?"

Pushing out a sound that was half laugh, half resigned sigh, Colin walked over to the door, snagging the keys off the hook that'd been there probably from long before he was born. "Somebody needs to hold the dog. And it'll be quicker since I actually know where the clinic is. So come on. Unless…" Against his better judgment he gave her outfit a cursory glance. Okay, maybe not so cursory. "You want to change?"

She *pff*'d. "I think as long as I'm not naked, I'm good." And, yep, she blushed again. "What I mean is…"

"I know what you mean," Colin said, swinging open the door and handing back the pup as she walked through it, and her scent walloped his senses, making all those hormones laugh their little hormoney butts off.

Clinging to the bandaged-up pup wearing his Cone of Shame, Emily climbed back in the car, waiting while Colin chatted with his brother, who'd followed him out of the clinic. Hard to believe they were related, frankly, Zach's slender build and straight dark hair making him look nothing like big, solid, curly-headed Colin, a beard-hazed cherub on steroids. It was good, though, to see Colin actually laughing as he talked with his brother, and the genuine guy hug they exchanged before Colin got back behind the wheel.

"You shouldn't have done that," she said, earning her a frown as he rammed the key in the ignition.

"Hugged my brother?"

She rolled her eyes. "No. Paid the bill. Especially since I suckered you into going to the vet with me."

"Is that what you did? Suckered me?"

The humor in his voice made her feel better than it should have. "Whatever," she muttered, and he actually laughed. He backed out of the space in front of the office, then turned toward the center of town, glancing over at the dog. Who, clearly worn-out from his ordeal, had passed out in her lap.

"How's he doing?"

"How do you think?" she said, and Colin chuckled again. But other than a sprain and a fairly minor wound, probably caused when the poor dog got dumped, he was fine. Or would be, once he got fattened up a bit. Although who was going to be doing the fattening hadn't been decided yet. Male, about eight weeks, unchipped—no surprise there—indeterminate breed. Wasn't going to be small, though, Zach had guessed. Emily frowned. "Who'd get rid of a dog they'd already had for a couple of months? And why at the ranch?"

Beside her, big shoulders shrugged. "Maybe it wasn't the original owner. Maybe whoever'd been given the dog decided they didn't want him, figured the ranch was as good a place as any to leave him."

"I can't even imagine." Lowering her stinging eyes to the pup, she toyed with one silky, floppy ear. "At least when I had to give up my dog," she said through a constricted throat, "I made sure he went to a great home. I didn't simply dump him somewhere and leave it to fate."

A moment's silence preceded, "You had to give up your dog?"

"Yeah," she breathed out, facing out the windshield again. The puppy whooped in his sleep, making her smile.

"This little mutt I'd rescued after I first moved into my own place. Barnaby. But Michael was allergic."

"Ah."

Amazing, how much meaning the man could cram into a single syllable. Despite the tightness in her chest, Emily smiled. "It made sense at the time. And it was an open adoption. I get pictures. Updates. He seems happy enough. Especially since now he has kids to play with. But my point is, if I had any idea who tossed this one like he was a piece of trash, I'd rip 'em a new one—"

Colin's stomach rumbled so loudly the pup lifted his head.

"Sorry," Colin muttered. "I hadn't bothered with breakfast, and then you showed up with fuzzy-butt there, and..." He shrugged. His stomach growled again, making the puppy yip and growl back. Sort of.

"Okay, that's settled," she said. "You know where Annie's is?"

"Of course I know where Annie's is—"

"Good. Then let's go. Since the least I can do is feed you, after everything you've done. Unless you really need to get back right away?"

"No, that's... I mean..." His hand tightened around the wheel. "Now that you mention it, I could eat my weight in tamales right about now. And it's not as if I'm on a time clock or anything. I can stay up all night to catch up if I want. So...sure. Why not?"

Then he tossed a brief grin in her direction and she thought, *And you've gone and done it now, girl, haven't you?* Although what, exactly, she'd gone and done, she wasn't entirely sure. But whatever it was, her own stomach was fussing up a storm, too. And not from hunger. Not that kind of hunger, anyway. And yet his accepting her offer pleased her beyond all reason.

Not to mention that smile.

Honestly. The man was the world's suckiest curmudgeon.

"So you know Annie's?" he said.

"Since one of your sisters-in-law works there, I most certainly do," Emily said as they pulled into an empty space in front of the diner, across from the town square. But even after cutting the engine, Colin stayed behind the wheel, one hand resting on the top as he stared out at the nondescript whitewashed building. Shadows from the trees in the square, however, flickered across the giant plate glass window, as well as the trio of small tables and chairs set up to take advantage of the warmer weather, lending, if not exactly *charm*, at least a certain comfortable unpretentiousness that was very appealing. Especially considering the slew of fancier restaurants in town that catered more to the ritzy ski resort patrons than locals. But that was just it: while the pricier places might make their clients feel indulged, Annie's Diner made a person feel like family. As though you'd come home. Emily liked that.

Unbuckling her seat belt, she cast a sidelong glance at Colin and asked, "When was the last time you were here?"

"Too long," he said on a telltale sigh.

Emily shifted the puppy, who'd conked out again. "We certainly don't have to eat here, if you don't want to. I hear that new Asian fusion place is pretty good. Although we'd probably have to leave the dog in the car—"

"What? No, this is fine. And I somehow doubt I can get tamales at the Asian place." Finally, he unbuckled his own seat belt. "But we should probably eat outside. Because of the dog. If it's warm enough, I mean."

In the sun it was. Emily set the sleeping dog on one of the unused chairs, swiveling it around to make a nest between the building's wall and her purse, which she'd grabbed before they'd headed into town. Not ten seconds later, however, they heard a muffled shriek from inside the restaurant, followed by one very excited Annie barreling outside, arms outstretched and babblings of joy tumbling like a waterfall from her mouth. Whatever Colin's reason for leaving Whispering Pines, it sure wasn't because nobody liked him.

The small woman yanked him into her arms, held him back, cackled out, "Holy hell, it's really you!" then yanked him back down again, wisps of her salt-and-pepper hair escaping her messy bun. And Colin, bless his heart, hugged the woman back. She released him again, smacked his arm, then folded her arms across her flat chest, shaking her head. "I'd about given up on ever seeing you again. What brings you back now, after all this time?"

Almost grateful for her apparent invisibility, Emily wondered if Annie noticed the change in Colin's expression, like a lightbulb not firmly seated in its socket. Huh. "Working on a book," he said, his hands stuffed in his back pockets. "Figured this was as good a place as any."

She also caught a flicker of skepticism—as though she didn't quite believe him—in the older woman's expression before she lit up again. "You may not know this, but your mama and daddy are real good about keeping everybody in the loop, showing off your work to anyone who'll stand still long enough for them to shove it in their face. Whole town's proud of you, boy."

Adorable blush, Emily thought a moment before Annie seemed to realize Colin wasn't alone. "Oh, my word, Emily—I didn't even see you sitting there! I'm so sorry! Didn't know you were back in town. But…wait." Confusion blossomed in her eyes for a moment as she looked back and forth between Colin and her. "Did you two come together?"

Emily laughed. "Long story. And solely because of this guy," she said, pointing to the puppy.

"What on earth...?" Her arms still crossed, Annie came closer. "Where did this little thing come from?"

"The ranch. Somebody abandoned him there, we think. So we brought him to Zach to get checked out." Emily bent at the waist to cup the little guy's head inside the cone. "Now we have to figure out what to do with him. I do, anyway. Since I found him."

Annie shot her a look that said her "answer" had only provoked five times more questions. About what, Emily could only guess. But all Annie said was "Meaning you don't want to keep him."

"It's not that I don't want to, it's just...that would be tricky. Since, well, my life's kind of all knotted up right now."

"What with you getting married, you mean."

"Um, actually..." Emily said, and Annie let out a soft groan. Because women understood these things before they were said out loud.

"Oh, honey...no."

"Yep."

"I'm so sorry." The older woman leaned over to pull Emily into a hug before looking back up at Colin. "And I'm guessing you can't take the dog, either."

His brow furrowed, he glanced over at the puppy. "Since I'm rarely in one spot longer than a few weeks... no. I can't. But maybe Josh and Deanna will take him."

"They might at that. If not, I'll be happy to put the word out, see what comes of it." Annie looked back down at the dog, chuckling as he twitched in his sleep. "Sweet little guy. Somebody's gonna love you, for sure. And for goodness' sake, y'all don't have to stay out here if you don't want to! Charley Maestas brings his dog in here nearly every day, nobody cares. Least of all AJ and me."

Colin chuckled. "Isn't there some kind of ordinance against that, unless it's a service dog?"

Annie swatted away his objection. "I won't tell if you won't. Unless you two would prefer to dine alfresco?"

"Actually..." Emily lifted her face to the sun, enjoying its sweet caress, a welcome reprieve from the bitterly cold spring winds that had assaulted the landscape every day since she'd come. "I wouldn't mind. But it's up to you," she said to Colin.

Whatever was going through his head, she had no idea. Although she was guessing quite a bit, judging from the look in those weirdly light eyes.

"Out here's fine," he said, a sudden breeze ruffling his curls.

Which oddly made *Emily* shiver.

Chapter Four

"You sure?" Emily said, and Colin tamped down the sigh a nanosecond before it escaped. Because hell no, he wasn't sure. Of anything, to be honest. On the one hand, there'd be other people inside. Other conversations, other noise, other distractions. Out here, it'd just be the two of them. And a comatose dog in a cone. Not much of a chaperone.

"Positive. Since now that I'm out..." He glanced toward the park across the street, where a host of dripping cottonwoods, their branches laden with the beginnings of their electric green summer attire, seemed to worship the clear blue sky. *Innocence*, he thought, wondering where the hell that had come from, before returning his gaze to Emily's and seeing much the same thing there. Or...not? "It occurs to me I've been cooped up too long."

"All righty, then," Annie said—hell, he'd nearly forgotten she was there—then she took their orders: tamales and refried beans for Colin, a BLT for Emily. Colin waited to sit until after Annie went back inside, where they heard her bark their orders to her husband, AJ. Emily grinned, then leaned over to soothe the tiny beast, quivering in his sleep, and something clenched in his chest.

"I still can't believe your fiancé made you get rid of your dog."

Not that it was any of his business what'd gone on between this woman he barely knew and some dude he didn't know at all. But Colin couldn't help it, he had real issues with one member of a couple dictating what the other could and couldn't do. Or at least making them feel bad about it. Meaning from the moment she'd told him about her dog, annoyance had latched on to his brain worse than a goathead sticker.

Emily's brows lifted, disappearing underneath those wispy, goldish bangs as Annie swept out, plunked down two glasses of iced tea and straws, and disappeared again. After a moment Emily pinched three fake sugar packets from the container on the table, ripped off the tops and dumped the crystals into her tea. "I told you," she said as she stirred, "he was allergic."

"There's stuff you can take for that, you know."

Her spoon clanked when she set it on the saucer. "He tried, actually. It made him too sleepy to function. And I think that's called compromise." She took a sip of the tea. "Or don't you believe in that?"

"Compromise is working out an agreement where nobody loses. In my book, anyway."

The pup twitched in his sleep; Emily picked him up, tucking him under her chin. Not easy with that damn plastic thing around his neck. Colin could have sworn the dog grinned. "Is that even possible?" she said, her gaze touching his. "I mean, aren't there inevitably going to be times when somebody has to capitulate? Besides, it was only a dog."

Except, judging from her voice's slight quaver, it was a pretty good guess her words weren't exactly lining up with whatever was going on in her head. Not that he didn't know—all too well—where she was coming from. A thought that was clearly hell-bent on resurrecting old regrets of his own.

Like his agreeing to this meal, for one thing. Colin lifted his own tea to his mouth, took a long swallow. "Like hell," he said softly, setting down the glass, "that it was *only* a dog. And in any case…"

"You don't have to say it," she said with a short, harsh laugh. "But at the time, the dog was the only issue—" Clamping her mouth shut, she shook her head. "I can't believe I was such an idiot." Then she shoved out a short, dry laugh. "Or that you'd be even remotely interested in the soap opera that's been my life lately."

A waitress—young, pretty, perky—appeared with their food, setting down the piled-high plates with a flourish before bouncing back inside. Colin picked up his fork and attacked the tamales. As in he ripped them to shreds. As much as part of him wouldn't mind doing that to Emily's ex. Ignoring the last part of her comment—because as long as they talked about her, they weren't talking about him— he said, "And I'm gonna stick my neck out here and say it wasn't you who was the idiot." At least that got a little laugh. "Hell, Emily—everybody makes mistakes," he said quietly. "Bad choices. Don't beat yourself up."

His face heated. And not only because of the hot-as-hell tamales. And what with them sitting out here in the sun…he was pretty sure she noticed.

But all she did was set the puppy back on the chair and pick up her overstuffed sandwich to take a huge chomp, sending mayonnaise squirting down her chin. Unfazed, she wiped up the mess with her napkin, then sat back in the chair, her arms folded across her ribs as she chewed. Thinking, no doubt. As one did when they had a brain. Which this gal obviously did.

"Yeah, well," she finally said after she swallowed, "giving up the *dog* was the least of it."

Colin frowned. "What else?"

"Teaching." She picked up the sandwich again and took another, neater, bite. "Kindergarten. Because Michael didn't think I should work."

"And what century is this again?"

Her mouth twisted. "His family is ridiculously traditional. Even more than mine, which is saying something." She stared at her plate for a long moment before saying, "It's funny how people assume if you grow up privileged, for lack of a better term, that you're spoiled." Her eyes lifted to his, the space between her brows pleated. "Especially if you're an only child. Not that it's not true, at least on the surface. Certainly I always had whatever I needed. And got a lot of what I wanted. To pretend otherwise would be disingenuous. But weirdly what made me happiest wasn't the stuff, it was making sure everybody *else* was happy."

"Even if that meant giving up something that was so important to you?"

Yep, he might've sounded a little pissed there. If Emily noticed, however, she didn't let on.

"Apparently so," she sighed out. "So naturally it made sense to carry that mind-set into my marriage. Although to give myself some credit, I figured I could talk him into letting me go back into teaching after we got married. So dumb." Her mouth screwed up again. "Sorry."

"S'okay," Colin said, shoveling in another bite of his

lunch. Breakfast. Whatever. "Like I said, you're hardly the first person to…"

"Screw up?"

A dry chuckle pushed from his chest. "Funny how it's a lot easier to tell someone else not to beat themselves up than it is to take your own advice."

"Truth," she said, lifting her tea in a mock toast. Then she frowned. "Nobody's perfect, you know? And Michael and I were attuned to each other's quirks, I suppose. We…" Her eyes met his. "Things were okay between us. Okay enough, anyway."

"Aside from the dog. And his making you give up your career. And his screwing around on you."

Another short laugh pushed through her nose. "When you put it like that…" She finally took a swallow of her tea. "I guess I figured the pluses outweighed the minuses. Well, until the final bombshell, which pretty much cleared the scoreboard. But in the beginning…oh, my gosh, our parents were *thrilled*. In fact, I think they were more caught up in the fairy tale than I was. The socialite's daughter marrying a US senator's son…cue the happy Disney critters flinging sparkly confetti, right?"

Colin almost smiled, but only because Emily did. "When did you find out?"

"About the cheating?" She took another bite of her sandwich. "A few weeks ago. By accident. He'd left his phone out, and I caught part of a text I doubt he'd expected me to see." Colin's brows slammed together. "Not the brightest move in the world. On his part, I mean. Although considering how relieved he looked when I confronted him, frankly I think he let things slip on purpose. Especially when he said that, actually, things would be easier now that I knew."

"Easier? For whom?"

"Exactly," she said. Only this time, he heard—saw—the

scarring behind the innocence. Not to mention a worldliness he wasn't sure how he'd missed. Recently acquired though it may have been.

"And how long were you two together?"

"Three years. I know. Although he *swore* they 'only' reconnected in the last year or so." Her mouth twisted. She looked back at the dog. "In every meaning of the word *reconnected*." She met his gaze again. "He actually promised it was over," she said, then *pff*'d a little laugh. "As if I'd actually believe him? Not hardly. Oh, and it gets better. It's someone *else* he's apparently known since college. An old girlfriend. Or something."

Shrugging, Emily picked up her sandwich again, poking a bit of bacon back inside the bread before taking another bite.

"You seem amazingly calm about the whole thing."

She *pff*'d again. "I'm nothing if not a product of my upbringing. Never let 'em see you sweat and all that. Inside, though, trust me—it feels like a nest of pissed-off rattlesnakes. Especially since…"

This time, her blush was so furious Colin briefly wondered if she was okay.

"Emily?"

But she shook her head. "Never mind."

And Colin thought he'd wanted to smack the guy senseless *before*. Yes, despite having no clue what lay behind that *never mind*. Because her red cheeks said it all, didn't they? At least, enough. Worse, though, was the realization that his impulse to inflict bodily harm stemmed from something way deeper than simple protective instinct.

And far, far more scary.

"What I don't get is why?"

Her forehead crimped. "I didn't see the signs?"

"Signs? What *signs*?" Colin reached for her hand, having to take care not to crush it, he was so damned mad. "For God's sake, you're not supposed to be looking for *signs* from somebody you *trust*, okay? No, what I meant was…" He let go to cross his arms over his chest. "Why on earth would this dipwad think he could get away with it?"

At least that got her to smile. "I guess because he knew rocking the boat wasn't my style, that…" Her mouth pulled flat. "That I'd do almost anything to not embarrass myself. Or the people I felt I owed."

Owed. What an odd word choice. "Except they all overestimated how far you could be pushed."

She gave him a funny look, a tiny smile poking at the corners of her mouth. "Apparently so. *Especially* once I had all the facts. I might be a people pleaser, but I'm not a masochist, for crying out loud. So strangely I'm actually very grateful for how things played out. Because if I hadn't found out when I did…" Another breath left her lungs. "I can't even imagine the hell that would have been. For any of us, frankly. And I am here to tell you, this chick's doormat days are over. And they probably wouldn't be if none of this had happened."

Only the fierce determination in her eyes was clearly wrestling with what Colin could clearly see was raw heartbreak, that somebody she'd loved—or in any case believed she had—had been lying to her for at least a year, probably longer. Maybe his situation hadn't been exactly the same, but he knew, too, what it felt like, that breath-stealing sensation of having been catapulted into an alternate dimension when you suddenly realized you were in a relationship based on dust—

And seeing the tangle of emotions on Emily's face provoked another spurt of protectiveness. Which was the last thing she probably wanted, and *definitely* the last thing he could afford to feel right now. If ever. But a weird…pride, he guessed it was, flickered in there somewhere, too, that despite her obvious mortification, no way was she going to be, or even play, the victim. Not now, or ever again.

Because this was no child, not by a long shot, but a woman…one whose newfound inner strength was a force to be reckoned with.

A realization that only shined a big bright light on why Colin needed to ignore the physical tug more than ever. Because she'd been used before. And he'd been had. So no way was he even going near that road again, for both of their sakes. But especially hers, he thought, as a family with two young kids passed their table on their way into the diner, and the little girl—four or five, maybe—went nuts over the puppy.

"You can pet him if you like," Emily said, heaving the sleepy little thing up so the kids could get to him, her chuckle warm at the little girl's giggles when the pup nibbled her fingers.

"What's his name?"

"He doesn't have one yet—"

"Why's he wearing that thing around his neck?" the child asked, her face scrunched into a combination of curious and concerned.

"So he won't mess with the bandage around his boo-boo. It's only for a week or so, though. Otherwise he's fine. And we're actually looking for a home for him," Emily said to the kids' parents, grinning. "You interested?"

The mother laughed. "Oh, gosh, sorry—we've already got as many animals as we can handle. But as cute as he is, I doubt you'll have any trouble placing him. Come on, guys," she said to the kids, steering them inside before her resolve crumbled, Colin was guessing. But she smiled back at Emily. "Good luck!"

"So what's the plan?" he asked Emily as she settled the pup into her lap again. "For you, I mean. Not the dog."

"No earthly idea. Although I suppose go back to DC, start the job search. I can probably get another teaching position, if I want it."

"Do you?"

"More than anything. I'm crazy about little kids."

Colin thought of how her voice had gentled as she talked to the little girl, and his own gut cramped. "I kinda got that impression. Private school?"

Her eyebrows shot up. "No. Public. Why would you assume private? Never mind," she said when he flushed, realizing his gaffe. "Don't answer that." Then she snorted. "As close to rebellion as I ever got, first wanting to go into early childhood education, then wanting to work with kids who wouldn't necessarily be 'easy.' Who maybe hadn't had many of the advantages I'd had."

Colin linked his arms high on his chest. "Kind of a sweeping indictment of the public school system, isn't it?"

"More true in the areas I asked to teach than you might think."

"Why?"

A small smile touched her lips, as though she completely understood his question. "Because I saw it as some small way to make a real difference. And yes, I realize a lot of people would call it rich person guilt. Or worse. It's not, though. At least, I hope it's not. God knows my idealism got taken down a peg or ten my first year, but…" Her brows pushed together. "But it got replaced by something much more solid. Much more real. I honestly loved teaching, even on those days when I wondered what the hell I'd gotten myself into. Seriously, if it was just ego stroking I was after, I can think of a lot easier ways to earn a living. Not to mention more lucrative ones."

Smiling, Colin thought of his own work, how he'd grav-
itated toward chronicling the struggles of those whose
lives were defined by them. The more he worked on his
book, the more he itched to get back to what his father had
rightly identified as his calling. His purpose.

Even as that collided with another, long neglected—
and even longer denied—pull he could no longer ignore
toward the very place he once couldn't leave fast enough.
And which made it even more imperative he ignore the
equally magnetic pull from the direct blue gaze across
from him. A pull he doubted Emily even realized she was
exerting. Especially given her situation.

"So you'll go back home?"

The question seemed to startle her, even though she'd
said virtually the same thing seconds before. Emily looked
down, chuckling at the blob of tomato that had landed on
her chest. She plucked it off, dropped it back on her plate.
"*Home* is very important to me. I'm a definite nester. And
not gonna lie, one of the things I was most looking forward
to was making that nest with Michael, having a couple of
kids of my own…" She tossed one hand in the air. "Turning
people's heads with my remarkable ability to effortlessly
balance motherhood and career, being the gracious hostess
as well as…" Another blush stole across her cheeks. "The
perfect wife," she finished softly, then snorted again. "A
total crock, but there you are. And now…"

The waitress reappeared to clear their places; Emily
asked for the check, then gathered her purse off the side-
walk to dig out her wallet. Colin couldn't help but notice
her pretty hands, the gleaming polish on each perfect nail,
the flawlessness marred only by a slight indentation where
her engagement ring had been. He wondered if she'd returned it, only to immediately decide of course she had.

"And now I have to totally reassess what that word means. Where home really is. *What* it is."

"But you just said—"

The pup looked up when the waitress returned with the charge slip for Emily to sign. Tucking her copy of the receipt into her purse, she met Colin's gaze again. "I know what I just said. But I guess you could say things are kind of…fluid right now." She chuckled. "For the first time in my life, I have no one and nothing to answer to. I can do whatever I damn well please. For a while, anyway, until my savings run out." Then, frowning, she looked over at the dog. "And what are we going to do about you, little guy?"

Her genuine concern for the dog, the light shining in her eyes for the little girl a few minutes ago… What kind of creep stomps on a heart that big?

Or worse, takes advantage of it?

Colin got to his feet, plucking the pup off the chair. "Between my three brothers and my parents, I don't imagine we'll have any problem finding a home for him."

The chair squawked against the rough pavement when Emily pushed it back, then stood. "I suppose you're right," she said, even though the look on her face said she wasn't nearly as down with that idea as he would've expected. Despite her trying to pawn the dog off on perfect strangers not five minutes before.

But what he really hadn't expected was how bad that made him feel. Mainly because he was in no position to do anything for anyone to make them happy. Or even feel better. Especially some sweet young thing who'd been not only dumped, but dumped on. And it'd only taken a single lunch to come to the conclusion that Emily Weber's goodness ran soul deep, like some pure, unquenchable river of life.

A river he didn't dare even think of drinking from.

No matter how thirsty he was.

* * *

Chuckling, Emily sat cross-legged on the tiled floor in the ranch house's giant, beamed great room, watching the wriggling, growling little dog play tug-of-war with Josh's almost-five-year-old son, the cone no impediment whatsoever to puppy shenanigans. A breath of fragrant, sunshine-warmed air swept across her face, making her turn toward the open French doors. Soon the high desert evening would suck all the warmth out of the glorious day, but for now she was simply grateful for a sweet, peaceful moment. As was her cousin, Emily guessed when she glanced over to see Dee curled up in the corner of one of the room's leather sofas, her lips curved in a blissful smile as she watched the pup and boy tussle. Josh was out doing chores and baby Katie napped, clearly oblivious to both the pup's yapping and Austin's nonstop, high-pitched giggling.

"I'm really sorry we can't keep him," Dee said for what felt like the hundredth time since Emily showed up with the dog three days before. "But between the baby and getting the gallery set up—"

"It's okay, Dee, really. You don't have to keep apologizing."

"Not that he's not adorable, but training a puppy takes so much time and energy—"

"Dee!" Despite the knot in her stomach Emily strongly suspected had less to do with finding a home for this dog than…other things, she smiled. "I get it." And she really did. Being awakened by a teething baby several times a night was clearly wreaking havoc on the whole family, whether Dee would actually admit that or not. "Sheesh."

But Deanna still looked all verklempt. Probably because, between imminently arriving new babies and wedding planning and the like, none of the other likely candidates could take him, either. Of course, Annie had put up a sign in the diner, as had Zach at the clinic, so Emily felt pretty confident the little hound wouldn't be homeless for long. And Dee did say that as long as Emily was around to take care of him, he could stay there until a more permanent solution was worked out. Although of course the problem with that was she'd only become more attached, wouldn't she?

Seeming to realize she was *right there*, the baby dog swung around and came bounding over in a burst of un-coordinated canine joy to clamber into her lap, where he planted his oversize paws on her chest to give her chin a thorough wash.

Austin folded up onto the floor to smush up beside her, smelling of dirt and sunshine and tangy little boy, and Emily's heart twisted with missing being around "her" kids. "He really loves you, huh?" he said, pressing closer so he could pet the dog, who of course immediately decided the boy's face needed washing, too.

Emily laughed. Then sighed.

Because reassessed goals or no, she was getting real tired of falling in love with things she had to eventually give up—or give up on. A realization that didn't keep her from gathering the pup closer, laughing again when he then started nibbling at the ends of her loose hair.

"I think it's safe to say he loves everybody," she said, planting a kiss on the little boy's messy curls. Life here was loud and crazy and frequently dirty, and the chaos wrapped around Emily's wounded heart like one of baby Katie's soft little blankets. *Perfect*, she decided, was not only unachievable, it was boring—

She laughed when, as she gently tugged on the puppy's velvety ears, Dumbo-style, he swung his head from side to side in a futile attempt to bite her fingers.

"Josh said Thor's old crate is in the tack room," Dee

said. "That might help. Temporarily, I mean." Emily looked up to see apology in her cousin's eyes. "Because between a squealing baby—" as if on cue, Katie's feed-me wail floated out from the baby monitor on the coffee table "—and an overenthusiastic little boy," Dee said with a pretend glower at her stepson, who grinned, "he probably needs his sanctuary."

And despite what Josh had said to her that first night, her bringing in a dog hadn't been part of the game plan.

"Sorry—"

"It's okay, honey, we'll work it out." The wailing became more frantic. "Really."

Yawning, Dee shoved off the sofa, wobbling a bit as she tugged down her long-sleeved T-shirt. Then she held out her hand to Austin. "Wanna come help me change her diaper?"

The little boy made a face, but took Dee's hand anyway, and followed her to the baby's room. Emily let her head fall back against the sofa cushion, shutting her eyes as, with a huge doggy sigh, the puppy promptly passed out.

Sanctuary.

Like the ranch, the town, was to Emily. Had been, anyway, until that lunch with Colin. She wasn't used to men directly meeting her gaze, she'd realized. Not her father, certainly. Or any of her other boyfriends, pre-Michael. And then not Michael, either, at the end, when he must've been suffocating under the weight of all those lies. Hell, yeah, she was still angry with him. But that would wear off, eventually, leaving in its wake an ocean of pity. Because in the long run, it'd be the dirtbag who suffered. Not her.

And either of those were preferable to whatever the heck feelings these were, provoked by that mountain of steely calmness she'd shared lunch with the other day.

A mountain in which were buried all manner of secrets, she suspected. Not national-security-threatening secrets, no—or at least, she didn't imagine—but the kinds of secrets men like that would take to their graves rather than getting all touchy-feely-sharey.

And she'd had enough secrets to last a lifetime, hadn't she?

Her phone dinged—the alarm she'd set to tell her when her brownies were done, since the kitchen was too far away to hear the buzzer. Setting the pup back on the floor, she heaved to her feet and plodded barefoot down the hall, the sweet, heady scent of warm chocolate intensifying as she got closer to the kitchen. It was the fifth batch of brownies she'd made since her arrival, but tough. It wasn't as if she had a wedding gown to fit into anymore, was it?

Although she might want to still fit into her jeans.

Granted, the kitschy kitchen wasn't her style—the hand-painted Mexican tiles were too busy for her taste, the cabinets and floor too dark—but it practically vibrated with Josh and Deanna's contentment. With…*promise.* Deanna's father leaving the ranch to her and Josh equally had been a shock, Emily knew. But for all her uncle's faults, not to mention the mistakes he'd made with his only child—more from cluelessness than malice, it turned out—Granville Blake had definitely gotten one thing right: bringing Dee and Josh together again, even though he'd deliberately separated them as teenagers.

An outcome that gave Emily hope, even as she had to battle hair-singeing envy every time she saw the happy, but exhausted, couple together.

"You do realize you're seriously sabotaging my attempts to get rid of the baby weight, right?" Dee said when she came in with the kids, the drooly, grinning baby slung on her hip like a sack of flour.

"Hey. I'm good with eating them all if that makes you feel better—"

"The hell you say," Dee muttered so Austin couldn't hear, settling into a chair at the huge kitchen table and yanking up her shirt to feed her child before thrusting out her hand. "Hand over the goods now and nobody gets hurt."

Chuckling, Emily cut a huge, gooey chunk of still-hot brownie from the pan, placing it on a napkin before setting it on the table beside Dee, then gave one to Austin, standing beside her with his nose practically in the brownie pan. "Don't let the puppy have any," she said. "Chocolate's not good for dogs."

Not that this was an issue, since after blowing on the brownie for maybe a second the kid basically inhaled the whole thing in two bites, crumbs dripping down his front. Which he caught and shoved in his already full mouth. "C'n I take the dog outside?"

"I suppose," Dee said. "But only out back. And stay by the back steps!"

"'Kay," the boy said, slapping his hands on his thighs to call the dog. "C'mon, boy! C'mon!"

And they were gone, although closing the back door behind them was apparently optional. Probably just as well, Emily thought, smiling again for her cousin. "You want milk with that? Or tea?"

Dee yawned, then nodded. "Milk. Please." Then, her forehead pleated, she lowered her gaze to her noisily feeding daughter. "I suppose we should think about what to feed your daddy for dinner, huh?"

Emily plucked a pecan off the brownies, stuffing it into her mouth. "Why don't you guys go out to eat?"

That got a weary chuckle. "Clearly you've never tried

taking a six-month-old to a restaurant. And Austin eats, like, a single nibble and he's done. It's kind of a waste."

Emily rolled her eyes. "Obviously I meant by your-selves, doofus. When was the last time you and Josh had date night?"

Dee looked at her as though she'd suggested they fly to the moon. "Um…never?"

Not that Josh's parents or brothers wouldn't be willing to take the kids. But hauling the kids to any of their houses, none of which were particularly close to the ranch, was a hassle. Same as it was for any of the brothers to bring their kids out to the ranch at night. And what with Josh's mom never knowing when she might be called out on a delivery, it was hard to rely on his parents, too. Heaven knew this family was joined at the hip, at least in theory. In practice, however, the more babies that got added to the mix, the more logistics weren't in their favor.

Add to that the fact that Josh and Deanna had never "dated" in the traditional sense before they got married, coming into it as they had with two kids already, and…

"Well, now's your chance," Emily said, scooping out a sizable brownie for herself. "No, I mean it—go into Taos, have dinner someplace other than Annie's, see a movie, stay out past your bedtime. My treat, even. And I'll watch the kids. We'll have brownies for dinner—" she stuffed a huge, melty glob of goodness into her mouth "—and watch the Cartoon Network until our eyeballs fall out." Then she laughed at her cousin's horrified expression. "I can follow directions, goose. And I know you've got breast milk in the freezer, so…" She shrugged.

Still, Deanna looked doubtful. Hopeful, but doubtful. "You sure?"

"If I can handle a whole class of five-year-olds, I think I can handle one and his baby sister. Or at least keep them alive until you get back. Besides, it's the least I can do to say thank you for letting me hang out here, all mopey and stuff."

Dee snuffled a little laugh. "You've hardly been mopey."

Not that she'd let them see, maybe. But there'd been more than one night when she hadn't been even remotely able to fend off the pity demons, nights when she'd cried herself to sleep, wanting so badly to be smart and strong and sure, wondering if she ever would. Never letting 'em *see* you sweat—or fall apart—didn't mean you didn't.

"Let me do this," she said. "Please. Let me feel…useful."

Tears glittered in her cousin's eyes as she extended one arm to Emily, pulling her into a hug that smelled of baby and breast milk and Dee's shampoo.

"I take it that's a yes?" Emily mumbled into her cousin's hair, and Dee nodded.

"Good," Emily said, letting go to finish cutting up the brownies, trying to ignore the beginnings of what felt an awful lot like panic.

Chapter Five

Colin heard Austin's shrieks before he rounded the last curve to the house, a sound that sent his heart into his throat and chilled his blood. Of course, then he felt like an idiot when he spotted the boy chasing the puppy and Thor in the front yard, the trio dodging the quivering shadows cast by a half dozen lush cottonwoods, shimmering gold in the setting sun. Then he caught Emily's laughter, as well, and his heart whomped inside his chest a second time. Only harder.

As in, like he'd been sucker punched.

Sitting on a blanket on the patchy grass with the baby, she shielded her eyes from the sun when she spotted him, then waved, grinning. Although even from this distance he didn't think he'd imagined the hesitancy in her smile. The caution. Only then she waved more insistently, beckoning him to join them. That surprised him, actually, considering there'd been no communication between them since that trip into town. Not that there should have been. Because reasons.

And if he'd had a lick of sense he could've waved back and pointed toward the cabin, indicating he had things to do. Only Austin started to wave, too, like he was flagging down a plane, and…well, it didn't feel right, ignoring his nephew. Especially since wasn't this a huge part of why he was here? To at least act like he had a family?

To figure out a few things?

So he hung a right and pulled into the house's driveway, trying like hell not to stare at Emily's flowing, sun-glazed hair, making her look like some damn Botticelli painting, *Venus on the Half Shell* or whatever. Except Venus was naked in the painting and Emily was wearing jeans and a loose sweater. Not sexy at all, let alone naked.

An image he maybe shouldn't dwell on too hard. Although the closer he got and the more her bangs looked like tiny sunbeams dancing across her forehead, the more that became a lost cause. Fortunately Austin came running up, plowing into Colin's legs with a big old grin splitting a face that reminded Colin so much of his daddy's at that age it was ridiculous. Ignoring the bittersweet ache permanently lodged, it seemed, in the center of his chest, Colin swung the little boy up into his arms, almost unable to process the child's immediate, uncomplicated acceptance of someone he'd never seen before a couple of weeks ago.

Although considering his other experiences, why should that surprise him?

"Daddy said you're living in our old house, huh?"

Colin smiled. "I am. For the moment."

"And he said that used to be his old house, too. When he was a kid?"

"Yep. Mine, too. And your uncles'. In fact, I shared a

room with your uncle Zach. The one at the back of the house."

The kid grinned. "That usedta be my room!"

"Get out!" He hoisted the solid little boy up higher in his arms. "In the bunk bed?"

"Uh-huh."

"Top or bottom?"

"Bottom. So all my friends could live on top. They liked it better up there, so I let 'em. Now they all live in a funny net in a corner of my room here. Except Monkey. Monkey lives on my bed."

Behind him, Colin heard Emily chuckle. He grinned for the little boy, even as his heart fisted so hard he wasn't sure how he was breathing. "The bottom was my bed, didja know that?" Austin shook his head. "And *now*—" he poked the boy's tummy, getting a squirmy giggle in response "—you and your daddy live in your stepmama's old house, from when she was a kid."

"I know, they said." The child linked his arms around the back of Colin's neck and gave him a very serious look. "Deedee said I can call her Mom, if I want. But I like Deedee. It's more special." He grinned again. "Like her!"

Thor kowtowed in front of them, tail wagging, barker barking…around the ball clamped in his mouth.

"Gotta go," Austin said, wriggling out of Colin's arms. "Thor wants me to play…"

And he was off, a blur of little boy limbs in the molten sunshine.

"You were actually out in the world again?" Emily teased from the blanket behind him, forcing him to face her. To face…stuff he didn't particularly want to. Because frankly he hadn't yet figured out how—let alone why— she was getting to him in ways he didn't want to be gotten to. And it wasn't only because she was pretty—he wasn't fourteen, for pity's sake—or even because he was lonely, even though that particular demon did occasionally sneak up on him, if he wasn't watching. But it still poked at him, how she told her story the other day, without even once playing the victim card.

"It does happen," he said, allowing at least enough of a smile to keep him from looking like he had a rod up his butt. "Sometimes I need to get out, get away from what I'm working on, take a walk. Go for a drive." No need to tell her why, that he'd been working on a series of photos that focused on one particular little boy he'd met in a refugee camp in Jordan, about a year ago. Right after Sarah. "Helps clear my head so I can be more objective when I go back to work. Josh and Deanna in the house?"

After a moment's speculative look, Emily smiled. "Nope. I kicked them out to give 'em some alone time with each other." The baby, sitting on the blanket in front of Emily, squinted up at Zach, giving him a drooly grin before jabbing her arms over her head, laughing at who-knew-what. Her own laugh even prettier than a nearby robin's trill, Emily grabbed Katie's chubby little hands, clapping them together. "I only hope they don't fall asleep in their food."

Colin felt a more genuine smile push at his mouth before looking out toward the mountains, the tops ablaze in the setting sun—a view he'd seen thousands of time growing up, that now provoked those old restless yearnings. Not for the same things, though, he didn't think. He let his gaze rest again on Emily, curled forward to touch her forehead to Katie's.

No, not for the same things at all.

Still holding his niece's hands, Emily straightened, a teasing grin on her lips. "Um…you could sit, if you want," she said gently. As though she knew what was going on in his head. Which was ridiculous for many reasons, not the least of which was that Colin himself wasn't sure what was going on in there. Just a lot of question marks, all tangled up like the fishhooks in his old tacklebox from when he was a kid. Another thought wedged itself in there, his father's "you are hopeless, boy" headshake when it'd take Colin twenty minutes to pry one free...

"You know," Emily said, letting go of the baby to wrap her arms around her knees. The breeze plucked at her hair; she shoved it back over her shoulder. "Enjoy the sunset. The moment?"

He nodded, mentally laughing at himself. Damn. For somebody who was supposed to be all about going with the flow, he felt about as fluid as cold molasses these days.

What the hell are you so afraid of?

His own voice, this time, prodding him to go places he wasn't ready to go. Not yet. Hell, maybe not ever. Still, right now, he was here. Meaning he could either accept the woman's simple invitation, or retreat to his hidey-hole for no real reason and let her think he had a screw loose. Not that he didn't, but no reason to let her think that.

So he lowered himself to the blanket, his heart turning over in his chest when a gurgling, jabbering Katie launched forward onto her belly and, with much grunting, tried her damnedest to army-crawl toward him.

"She crawls?"

"Not exactly," Emily said, chuckling when Colin leaned in to hook his hands under the baby's arms and lift her toward him. Squealing with delight, the kid slapped a slobbery palm against his cheek, then twisted to plop in his lap, where she released a victorious sigh before grabbing his hand and cramming it into her slimy mouth.

"Here," Emily said, tossing him a little blanket decorated in tiny teddy bears. "She does a great imitation of Niagara Falls these days."

"Thanks."

As he wiped drool off both him and the baby—ignoring her cries of protest—he caught Emily's smile.

"You're good at that."

"I've had practice," he said quietly, not looking at her. The rapidly chilling breeze swept across the yard, cooling the baby spit he'd missed on his hand.

Emily pulled up her knees again, linking her arms around them as she watched Austin and the dogs. "But obviously not with your own kids." Her gaze veered to his. "Or your brothers'."

"No."

Katie clapped her hands, chortling with glee at her brother's and the dogs' antics, and all the old instincts kicked in whether Colin wanted them to or not. Laughing himself, he turned the tiny girl around to let her push herself to her feet, her louder squeals apparently catching his nephew's attention. Austin and the dogs made a beeline for Colin, the boy barreling into his side like a linebacker, nearly knocking him and the baby over.

"Austin!" Emily yelled, lurching for him. "Watch out, sweetie—"

"It's okay, I've got him," Colin said, snaking one arm around the skinny little waist to halt the inertia while still hanging on to the babbling, oblivious baby. "But you need to be careful, buddy. You could've hurt yourself there. Or your baby sister."

His face instantly flaming, the little boy's gaze swung to the baby, as though suddenly realizing she was there. "Sorry, Katie!" He dropped to his knees, resting a grimy hand on the baby's back. "You okay?"

The tiny girl twisted toward him, bursting into a huge

grin when she saw her brother, then jutting one hand toward him.

"Yes, is the answer," Colin said, then met eyes the same color as his younger brother's. And yep, that was something almost like regret zinging through him, that he'd more or less missed out on the kid's life to this point. And not only his, but Zach's two, as well. Except being around these kids, who had families and *homes* and reasonably stable lives, only made him remember the bigger picture that had kept him away for so long. "Just don't want you to bump your noggin," he said, gently rapping his knuckles against the little boy's skull. The little boy giggled, making Colin's chest ache and his head hurt. Logically enough, considering all those twisted-up fishhooks in there.

Then the boy threw his arms around Colin's neck and gave him a hug, making him ache even more, before dashing off to play fetch with the big dog. The puppy, however, had stumbled over to collapse against Emily's knee, too pooped to pop. Or pup.

Colin set the baby back on her butt on the blanket and handed her a nearby toy, which she promptly crammed into her mouth. Then he nodded toward the passed-out puppy. "You name him yet?"

"Me?" She sounded startled. Looked it, too, wide eyes and all. Then she shook her head. "No. I'll leave that to whoever gives him his forever home."

"So why *can't* that be you? Nothing says you couldn't take him back to DC with you."

"Because my life is one big question mark right now? Or did you forget that part? As it is I'm probably going to have to turn him over to a shelter."

"What? Why?"

Playing with the puppy's ears, she gave a sad let's-be-a-grown-up-about-this shrug. "Because he keeps waking up at night, crying. And poor Dee and Josh get little enough sleep as it is, with babypie over there teething. I came out here to get away from my own problems, not to make more for Dee. Or your brother, who's a saint for letting me stay to begin with—"

"Then leave him with me," Colin heard himself say. At Emily's pushed-together brows, he added, "I don't sleep particularly well at night, anyway. And I'm sure we can find him a home long before…before I leave."

She looked back down at the pup, her mouth set.

"What?"

Her gaze glanced off his again before, with another shrug, she lowered it again to the pup. "I can't figure you out."

"That would make you a member of a very large club, then," he said, and she softly laughed. "So is that a yes?"

"To your taking the dog?" Another shoulder bump preceded, "Sure. In fact, it's an excellent solution. Since I'm in real danger of getting too attached."

"I can see that. Although…" Because if it was one thing he was good at, it was getting himself in deeper. "Feel free to come play with him anytime—"

"It's getting dark," Emily said, shivering as the streaks of red-gold light suddenly faded, instantly leaching the warmth from the air. She called Austin, then got to her feet and reached for the baby, chuckling as the child pumped her chubby little legs for all she was worth when Colin lifted her up. "Well." Settling the baby against her ribs, she nuzzled the downy head before meeting Colin's gaze again, yearning—as well as anger for what'd been snatched from her—leaking from her own. Although he doubted she realized how much. "If you're really serious about taking the dog—"

"Wouldn't've offered if I wasn't," Colin said, pushing himself to his feet, as well.

She nodded, shouldering a strand of hair away from her jaw. "Then you might as well come get his stuff. Food and bowls and…" She flushed. "Toys. Um, I might've bought a few. And Dee said there's a crate in the tack room that Josh used for Thor when he first got him. You might want that, too—"

"Hey, Uncle Colin," Austin said when he reached them, breathing hard as he scooped up the wriggling, licking puppy. "You wanna stay for dinner? There's lots!"

"Uh…thanks, but I don't think that's your invitation to give, dude—"

Shifting the baby higher into her arms, Emily laughed. "It's okay, he just beat me to it. It's what I call a 'whatever casserole.' It should be ready to come out of the oven about now, anyway. It might have identity issues, but it's good, I promise."

"An' there's brownies, too!"

"And there's brownies, too," Emily said, smiling. A little too hard, Colin thought.

"Emily made those." Austin grinned, giggling as he did his best to hang on to the pup. "They're like the best brownies, ever!"

At that, Emily laughed full-out. "Why, thank you, sweetie!"

Then she lifted those sweet blue eyes to Colin's again, sparkling over that smile, defying the sadness underneath, and between that and the promise of dinner he hadn't cooked himself *and* brownies, he might've lost his breath there, for a moment. Or his sanity. Hard to tell. But between those eyes and his nephew's hopeful expression… how could he say no?

"Sounds great," he said, swiping the blanket off the ground and shaking it out.

"You sure?"

"Absolutely."

But only that he was about to dive headfirst into shark-infested waters.

There was nothing sexier, Emily thought later when she walked back into the kitchen after putting the kids to bed, than a big man washing dishes. Especially one holding a spirited conversation with the tiny puppy gnawing his sneaker's shoelace at the same time. Choking back the laugh that wanted so badly to erupt, she stood in the doorway where he couldn't see her, simply watching. Absorbing. Smacking down the latest in an apparent series of wayward thoughts that seriously needed smacking.

Like, for instance, how watching Colin with the kids, his gentleness and humor, had stirred the cinders of three years' worth of hopes and expectations. Oh, she imagined—or at least hoped—she'd meet someone else one day, someone whose hopes and goals meshed with hers. Someone honest and true. Someone worthy of her, damn it. But that day, if it ever came, was way off in the future, after she'd had time to heal. To grow. To make sense of what had happened and make damn sure it didn't happen again.

So for *double*-damn sure she wasn't about to see Colin Talbot as anything except an exercise in proving her new-found strength. So let temptation flaunt itself in her face— no way in hell was she gonna bite.

He turned, startling her, his smile as careful as she imagined hers was. And despite her resolve, despite everything in her that said, "Uh-uh, honey," she wanted to know what his story was. What had put such caution in those pale eyes.

"There's coffee," he said, nodding toward the coffee-maker.

Meaning he was staying awhile? Interesting.

"Thanks." She crossed the tile floor, reached for a pair of mugs from the nearby cupboard. Somehow she didn't think it was her imagination, his gaze on her back. The questions floating in the air between them. Wanting to know more, knowing the folly of going there.

Coffee poured, she cradled the steaming mug to her chest and turned, chuckling at the pup's ferocious growl as he tried to kill the shoelace.

"You've made a friend." She lifted her eyes to his a moment before he squatted to pick up the dog. Thor had plopped in the dog bed by the pot-bellied stove near the oversize dining table, even though it hadn't been lit in days. Now the cat—who generally kept to himself when the kids were awake—plodded over to wedge herself beside the dog, who didn't seem to care one whit when her fluffy tail settled over his snout. "More than one, actually. The kids clearly adore their uncle."

Colin smiled—if you could call it that—as he cocooned the pup in his huge hands. But they weren't all chewed up and scarred, like his brothers'. "The feeling's mutual. Then again, it's not all that hard to make friends with most kids. Some, sure, have a real reason to be leery, but for the most part..." Shifting his gaze away from hers, he shrugged. "It's like their default setting is to be open. Loving." He set the pup back on the floor, shoving his hands in his pockets. "Before life hardens them, anyway."

Curiouser and curiouser. "I know what you mean," Emily said. "I think that's one reason I love teaching kindergarten. Getting them before their innocence gets scrubbed away."

Colin reached for one of the last brownies, stuffing half the thing in his mouth before adding, "These are terrific."

The thing was, after three years with Michael, if it was

one thing Emily was good at, it was spotting a prevarica-
tor…a skill more finely honed by hindsight, it turned out.
Unfortunately. But whatever Colin's reasons for switch-
ing the subject, they were none of her concern. So all she
did was shrug and say, "Can't take much credit, really,
they're from a mix. And I'm good at following directions.
But thanks anyway—"

A breeze shunted through the house when the front door
opened, bringing with it her cousin's laugh. A minute later,
Dee and Josh appeared in the doorway, hand in hand and
grinning like loons. Except then surprise swept across
both their faces when they realized Emily wasn't alone.

"I take it the date was a success?" Emily asked as Josh
crossed to his brother to clap him on his upper arm.

"Honey, just getting out of the house by ourselves was
a success," Dee said, slipping off her denim jacket and
hugging it to her middle. "But yeah…" She grinned over
at her husband. "It was good."

"Although I had this momentary panic," Josh said, "that
we'd discover we really had nothing to say to each other."

Emily laughed. "I take it your fears were groundless?"

"Hell," Josh said, grabbing the last brownie, then waving it toward his wife. "This one didn't shut up the entire
time."

"It's true," Deanna said with a *whatever* shrug. "Like
the dam broke, and all the stuff I either kept forgetting
to say or would fall asleep before saying came roaring
out. We probably won't have to talk again for at least two
months."

Another chuckle bubbled up from Emily's chest, this
time at how effortlessly the Westernized cadences her
cousin had worked so hard to eradicate from her speech
after she moved to DC had reasserted themselves. Gone,
too, was most of the chichi edginess Dee had appropriated

like a costume, leaving behind the Deanna Emily remembered from when they were kids. Only—she caught the wink her cousin gave her husband—much, much happier. Then Dee glanced behind her before giving Emily wide eyes.

"Both kids are asleep?"

"Wasn't that the plan?"

That got an exaggerated sigh. "For you, they both go to sleep. For us…" Her mouth twisted. Emily laughed.

"Beginner's luck, I assure you."

Dusting brownie crumbs off his fingers, which the puppy quickly scarfed up, Josh poked his brother. "So, what? You get roped into sharing the babysitting detail?"

Colin's chuckle sounded almost…relaxed. "Not exactly. They were all outside when I drove by, and long story short…your kid invited me to dinner."

"And you actually accepted?"

"I guess I did."

Dee huffed. "*How* many times over the past two weeks have I asked you to come eat with us and you'd come up with one sorry excuse after another about why you couldn't? I'm thinking maybe I should be offended. Especially since I know you had dinner with Zach and them." Except the light dancing in her eyes said she wasn't, really.

Although the flush sweeping over Colin's beard-hazed cheeks said…something. What, Emily wasn't sure. But then the exchanged glance between the newlyweds made her cheeks warm, too. Which was nuts.

"So Colin said he'd take babydog until we found a home for him," she said, probably too quickly. "And I told him you have Thor's carrier somewhere?"

That got another exchanged glance—these two were about as subtle as an explosion, yeesh—before Josh nodded, then turned to his brother. "I do. We can get it right now if you want."

"Uh...sure. Well..." Colin plucked the puppy, who was attacking his shoelace again, off the floor, as Josh gathered up bowls and dog food and such. "Thanks again. I'll...see you around, I guess."

Then they were gone. And, yep, Deanna turned narrowed eyes on Emily. "And would you like to fill me in before my imagination goes down untold murky paths?"

Emily snorted. "You don't honestly think his being here has anything to do with me?"

"Doesn't it? Only I'm sure I don't have to remind you—"

"That five minutes ago I was engaged to someone else. No, you don't. Although who was the one making all those untoward suggestions about taking advantage of still being, um, *prepared*?"

"And what part of 'I'm kidding' did you not get?"

Shaking her head, Emily snatched the brownie plate off the counter, swiping the crumbs into the trash before cramming it into the dishwasher. "Then before you and your imagination ride off into the sunset..." Buttons pushed, she shut the door, then turned, arms folded over her stomach, which was churning even more than the dishwasher. "It was like Colin said—Austin invited him to dinner, the man said yes. I was surprised, too, but I wouldn't read anything more into it if I were you."

"Because clearly you have no idea how huge this is."

"Dee. I doubt anything more's going on here than Colin's being lonely. Whether he'll admit it or not."

"Which would be my point?"

"Oh, for Pete's sake..." Emily blew out a breath. "Give me some credit, okay? I'm not about to..." Her eyes burning, she shoved her hair behind her ear. "I came out here to get my head on straight. That hasn't changed. Do I find Colin attractive? Sure—"

"At least you admit it."

"I'm burned, not dead. Look, I agree with you, that it was a big deal, his agreeing to have dinner with the kids and me. For reasons I'm not sure even he understands, let alone any of the rest of us. But if you think this has more to do with me than it did…that's nuts."

Her mouth pulled into the thinnest line possible without disappearing entirely, Deanna stared at Emily for a long moment before releasing a rough sigh. "It's just—"

"I know. And while I appreciate your concern…" Emily's eyes burned again. "I'd appreciate it more if you'd trust me enough to let me figure a few things out on my own. Damn it, Dee—the main reason I came out here was so I wouldn't have to listen to my *mother's* incessant harangue, to get away from her constant attempts to manipulate my life into some ideal that only existed in her imagination. Not that she didn't mean well, in her own obsessive-compulsive way, but even though I'd thought I'd broken away from her gravitational pull enough to live my own life, by moving out, by becoming a teacher…"

Emily gave her head another shake. "Clearly I hadn't nearly as much as I'd thought. I'm not an idiot, Dee. I know hooking up with Colin—or, frankly, anyone right now—would be insane and pointless. But how on earth am I ever going to learn how to navigate my own life without actually doing it? Without making my own decisions?" She pulled a face. "My own mistakes, if it comes to that. Which I'm sure it will. What with being human and all. But at least they'll be *my* mistakes. *My* choices. Not somebody else's. For once."

Her cousin crossed her arms. "So what you're saying is, you want the freedom to screw up?"

"Yes! Exactly! Because how else am I going to learn? To *grow*?" Her mouth twisted again. "To grow *up*."

After a moment, Dee crossed the space between them to tug Emily into her arms. "I'm sorry," she mumbled, then pulled away. "You're right."

A raw breath left Emily's lungs. "So no more fretting?"

Dee pushed a laugh through her nose. "Can't guarantee that, but..." One side of her mouth pushed up. "I'll keep my yap shut, how's that?"

"Thank you," Emily said, pulling her cousin into another hug. As victories went, it was a pretty small one. But she'd take it.

Even if she sounded a helluva lot braver than she felt.

Chapter Six

Cradling the little dog to his chest with one hand, Colin followed his brother into the "new" barn. And in an instant the familiar tang of hay and horse, the occasional soft whinny piercing a chorus of equine huffing, provoked feelings and emotions that were becoming increasingly difficult to parse the longer he was home.

Didn't help, either, that the damn dog smelled like Emily, which in turn brought to mind the look on her face when he'd taken the pup. Like a little kid trying so hard to be brave.

Except for the little kid part of that.

"I shoved the kennel in here somewhere," Josh said, his boots clomping against the concrete floor as he passed the stalls on the way to the tack room. There were actually three barns on the property—the original twenties-era structure, closer to the house and rarely used to house livestock these days; and another one like this, all metal and cement and modern amenities.

Colin counted a dozen or so horses in here, most of which ignored them as they passed, although a couple poked their heads over the stall doors, ears flicking in mild curiosity at the wriggling creature in Colin's hand. A particularly stunning roan mare gave a vigorous nod, inviting them closer. Colin obliged, feeling something ease inside him when she stretched her neck to first investigate the pup, then cuff Colin's shoulder. The puppy yipped, thrilled; the mare whinnied in response, then nodded again. Chuckling, Colin stroked her satiny neck for a moment before catching up to Josh, letting the puppy down. The dog promptly scampered off, nose to ground, trying to follow eighteen trails at once.

"Looks like you've got a full house," Colin said from the doorway to the tack room. It was pristine, save for one corner clearly used for storing all the junk not currently in use but too good to pitch. Including a collapsible wire kennel clearly intended for a much larger dog. Not something that weighed ten pounds. On a full stomach.

Josh tossed a grin over his shoulder as he jerked the kennel free of the detritus pile it'd been wedged in. "Gettin' there. Although about half of 'em are boarders. A couple rescues, too..."

He banged off the light and hauled the contraption from the tack room, clattering it onto the dusty floor in front of Colin before smacking his palms across his butt. The pup cautiously approached the kennel, stretching out as far as his little body would allow to sniff at it, only to jump back when the sole of Josh's boot scraped the floor. Laughing, Josh squatted to call the little guy over, reaching inside the cone to scratch one ear until he collapsed beside Josh's boot, tummy bared, to grin upside down up at Colin.

"And a couple of the horses are Mallory's, for her and

Zach's therapy facility. They hope to be good to go by June, did I tell you?"

"Zach did, when I was over there the other night." An evening filled with warmth and laughter…and silliness, he thought on a smile. Because three boys under the age of twelve, that's why. And dogs. And a redheaded spitfire who wasn't about to let a wheelchair clip her wings. Nor the events from her past that had put her in it. "It's good to see him so happy, after…everything."

His brother nodded, but not before Colin caught the squint. Not judgmental, maybe, but definitely questioning. Never mind that the minute he'd heard about the accident more than three years before that had taken his older brother's first wife, Colin had called Zach, saying he'd be on the first plane home if that's what Zach wanted. Except Zach had said no, there was nothing Colin could do anyway. A pretty typical Talbot response, actually, which Josh would realize if he thought about it for two seconds.

Colin was glad, though, that he'd be here for the wedding. He was glad he was here period, he realized as Josh stood and grabbed the crate again, making the puppy clumsily scramble to his feet. And if Emily Weber's presence had something to do with that… Shoot, if he could figure that one out, tackling world peace would be a piece of cake.

He took the crate from his brother to haul it out of the barn, even though they stopped along the way to chat with this or that mare, admire a colt, the pride radiating from his brother warmer than the sun in July. He knew Josh was thrilled to own, along with his wife, the ranch that had been the cornerstone of this part of New Mexico for more than a hundred years. But ranches of this size tended to be more of a financial drain than moneymakers these days, especially since Deanna's father had downsized the cattle end of things years ago.

"Which is why we're more grateful than we can say for Mallory's coming on board with her therapy facility," Josh said in answer to Colin's out-loud musings. Now outside, Josh slugged his hands in his back pockets. A weightless evening breeze nudged at them, the air chilled and somehow fruity, like a crisp white wine. The pup toddled ahead, only to plop his butt in the dirt and lift his snout, sniffing. "Between that and renting out the cabins down by the river during the hunting season, and the occasional rodeo winnings…" Josh shrugged. "We make do. And now that Dee's got her art gallery in town…" He grinned. "It's all about possibilities. Options."

"Or an awful lot of plates up in the air."

His brother chuckled. "Not gonna lie, we're talking risk with a capital *R*. But at least it's our risk to take, to try…" He huffed a sigh. "I know you never felt the connection to the place I did. It was the same with Dee, at least up until a few months ago. But for us, this is home. Simple as that."

As if anything was ever simple. Especially when it came to home and connections and who a person was. Where they were supposed to be.

"And if—"

"We're giving it two years," his brother said, lifting his gaze to a never-ending sky so choked with stars they bled into each other. Then his eyes lowered to Colin's again, shining with a determination that made him realize the goofy kid he remembered had long since left the building. Mostly, anyway. "Between us, we've got enough squirreled away to tide us over for that long while we figure out how to make this all work. Worst-case scenario? We'll sell it, find a smaller place, start over. The world won't end if it comes to that, believe me. But you better believe we're gonna do everything in our power to make sure it doesn't."

Now it was Colin's turn to look away, wondering, as he often did, what had tied most of his family to this place. Why his parents, his three brothers, had taken such firm root in this little corner of New Mexico, even if it'd taken Levi longer than the others, when Colin had wanted nothing more than to break free from it.

What was pulling him back now—

"You okay?" Josh asked, his brother's voice piercing Colin's thoughts.

"Just thinking about how all the stuff that seemed so black-and-white when you were a kid gets a lot more muddied as you get older."

"And I don't even want to know what you're talking about, do I?"

Colin pushed a laugh through his nose. "Probably not." Then he squinted back at the barn. "You doing all the work yourself?"

"Right now, it's still pretty manageable. It's nothing like when we were working cows, thank goodness. That was rough."

"I remember." He snorted. "There was a reason I left."

Actually, there'd been several. But 4:00 a.m. wake-up calls for most of the summer had definitely ranked right up there.

Josh chuckled. "Although I've got a couple high school kids who come after school and on weekends to help out. And Mallory's boy," he said with a grin. "Can't keep the kid away. Already got him training for barrels. Like his mama used to."

"He's, what? Eleven?"

"Nearly twelve. Perfect age. Mallory's probably gonna

need someone to help out with the facility, though, eventually. Especially somebody who's good with kids."

"The way everything else seems to be falling into place," Colin said quietly, "I'm sure that will, too."

His brother grinned over at him. "I'm sure you're right."

The dog trundled over, asking to be picked up. Colin obliged. Only now, of course, Emily's perfume mingled with the night's, poking at all those *feelings* again. At the yearning he'd refused to acknowledge for so long. Then he blew out a half laugh. "This family's positively exploding."

"Isn't it?" his brother said, sounding totally good with that. "Seriously doubt it's anywhere near done yet, either."

Colin frowned at his brother. "Is Deanna…?"

"What? Oh. No. Not that I know of, anyway. Sure, we'd like more kids down the line, but right now we've got our hands full with the two we've got. And the ranch and her gallery and everything. When the time's right. Speaking of whom, I should probably get back—"

"Right. Of course. Except…" The dog clutched in one hand, the kennel in the other, Colin said, "I already made sure Emily knows she can come see this guy—" he hefted the pup, who gave his chin a little lick "—anytime she likes. But it might not be a bad idea, her coming over tonight to help him get settled in."

Briefly raised brows gave way to a lopsided smile as his brother started back to the house, tossing a "Sure thing" over his shoulder as he strode off, his unasked question shimmering in the air between them.

Why?

Not that Colin could've answered, anyway, so thank goodness Josh hadn't asked. Except…a taste of her company had left him wanting more, was all. And considering her own situation, he sincerely doubted there was any danger of her reading anything more into the invitation than there was. Emily Weber was *safe*, in other words.

Whether he was, was something else entirely.

Emily was about to knock on the door when she realized Colin had left it ajar. Although because he was expecting her or he simply wasn't good at closing doors behind him, she had no idea. God knew Michael never had been, so maybe it was a guy thing. Who knew? So she knocked, anyway, telling herself the shiver that snaked up her spine at his deep "Come on in!" was due to the nippy night. Not her brain's having taken a hike to parts unknown.

Although since she was here—instead of, you know, acting like the big girl she was supposed to be and seeing the pup tomorrow or the next day—she supposed the brain-hiking thing was moot.

Still. She had to admit it was nice, being around a man who clearly had no agenda. Despite how he looked at her, as though he could see through to parts of her soul she hadn't discovered yet herself. Which by rights should be scary—

The puppy bounded up to her, a blur of bliss. And cone-free. Laughing, Emily picked him up, then looked across the room into that direct, greeny-gold gaze and lost her breath for a second.

—but oddly wasn't. Instead, she felt…safe. Why, she had no idea, since she barely knew the man. But damned if he didn't absolutely radiate integrity. Goodness. And something else she couldn't quite put a finger on, but that made her think, *Oh, okay. You'll do.*

For now, anyway. For this moment, when her brain was still muddled and her heart was shredded and she knew it would be a long, *long* time before trust and she resolved their differences. Right now, she needed *safe* and *good* and *integrity*.

And a puppy to cuddle, she thought, sinking cross-legged on the worn braided rug covering most of the living room floor to let the thing give her jaw a thorough washing. Dodging the little tongue, she looked around, taking in what looked like a leftover set from a Western movie, circa 1975—scuffed leather and dinged wood, faded geometric-design pillows, the small kitchen a study in murky greens and browns. She'd never been inside when she'd visited as a kid—no reason for her to have been, really—and now she found herself seeing it through Colin's eyes.

Apparently noticing her scrutiny, he chuckled. "It looks better in the daylight."

"I didn't—"

"You didn't have to. Want something to drink? Coffee? Tea?"

"No more coffee. I'll never sleep." She lowered her gaze to the dog. "You took off the cone?"

"The wound's as good as healed. I checked with Zach. He said it was okay. So, tea?"

"Sure. Although somehow you don't strike me as a tea person."

"Not usually, no. But I found some tea bags when I was cleaning out the cupboards. My mother's maybe? Have no idea how good they are, but—"

"Why'd you ask me to come over? Really?"

Halfway to the open kitchen, Colin turned, a frown etched between his brows. But instead of answering, he yanked an ancient kettle off the equally ancient gas stove, then said over the sound of water thrumming into it, "You want honesty?"

"If you wouldn't mind."

He clunked the kettle onto the burner and twisted on

the flame before facing her again, one hand curled on the edge of the counter behind him.

"I didn't invite you here because of the dog. He was just…convenient."

"I see."

His laugh, if one could call it that, matched his expression. "I doubt it. Since I sure as hell don't. But it's not about…" He blew out another breath. "I'm not trying to get into your pants, if that's what you're thinking."

"Actually," she grumbled, "considering my recent past, that would be refreshing." Then, at his puzzled look, she realized he had no idea what she was talking about. "As it happens, Michael became a lot less…attentive, shall we say, the last year or so we were together. He said it was because of his workload. Yeah, well, it was a *load*, all right."

Colin softly cursed, then crossed his arms over that nice, solid chest. "I'm sorry."

"So was I. Then. Now? Not so much."

"Even so, I take it you don't really mean that. That you'd—"

"Find it refreshing to be wanted? You bet. Even though it's equally refreshing that you don't. So figure that one out."

The kettle squealed. Colin snatched it off the stove and poured water into two mugs, tea bag strings dangling down their sides. "It's not that hard, really. You were not only rejected—" he crossed to where she was sitting, setting both mugs on the coffee table next to her before returning to the kitchen "—you were betrayed." He gathered spoons, a sugar bowl, a carton of half-and-half from the fridge. "So right now—"

The stuff now set on the table beside the mugs, he lowered himself to the floor in front of her, looking like the world's largest kindergartner. And he smelled like the wind, damn it. Michael, if she remembered correctly, had never smelled like the wind. Or anything else even remotely…earthy.

And he still hadn't answered her question, had he? About why he'd invited her over. Probably wouldn't, either. Then again, maybe he didn't really have an answer—

"So right now," Mr. Earthy was saying, "part of you wants nothing to do with men. And the other part of you probably wants nothing more than to get even."

Now it was her turn to laugh. Only to see her own pain reflected in his eyes.

"Speaking from experience?"

Nodding, he dumped two teaspoons of sugar into his tea.

"Recent?"

"Enough." He stirred the tea, setting the wet spoon on a napkin before slurping his tea. The dog abandoned her lap for his, only to disappear into the void made by his legs. A second later his little bewhiskered nose appeared over Colin's calves, then vanished again. "Although," Colin said, hoisting the pup back onto the floor between them, "the situation wasn't the same. The dishonesty, however, was."

With that, the light dawned that he *was* answering her question, in his own I'll-get-there-eventually way. Whether he realized it or not. But the upshot was the guy simply needed someone to talk to. Was it nuts, how flattered she was that he'd picked her?

That he trusted her enough to do that.

"She cheated on you?"

Another dry laugh shoved from his throat. "No. Although in a way it would've been easier if she had. At least that would've been cut-and-dried. But she wasn't upfront about how she really felt about my work. Not the work itself, exactly, but the fact that it kept us apart so much."

"And I take it she didn't want to go with you?"

"Nope. Not that I blamed her. I'm often in not exactly the safest places in the world. But what hurt the most was…" He glanced away, then back at Emily, his forehead crunched. "She never really understood why what I do was—is—so important to me."

"Did you ever tell her?"

"More times than I could count."

Emily shifted to relieve her numb butt. "And maybe," she said gently, "it's about telling the right person."

Colin watched her for a moment with those searing eyes before shoving himself to his feet and going over to an old desk wedged into a corner of the room. He seemed to hesitate, though, before grabbing a compact two-in-one computer/tablet combo and returning, lowering himself to the floor again and flipping the tablet open so the screen faced her. His gaze glanced off hers again before, slowly, he began scrolling through dozens of photos of children, some smiling, some crying, many whose faces radiated such fear and uncertainty Emily's eyes filled.

"Where…?" she finally said through a throat so tight she was surprised any sound came out at all.

"Various places." His voice was so low she could barely hear him. "Greece. Turkey. Jordan." He paused at one picture, a stunning black-and-white photo of a laughing little boy, the sun shimmering in his dark, straight hair. Emily stared for several moments at the photo, transfixed, before realizing how still Colin had gone beside her. She lifted her eyes to the side of his face—

Without thinking, she rested her hand on that strong, muscled arm, resisting the urge to stroke away the chill she felt there. "Who is he?"

"What? Oh." He seemed to shake himself free, then

shook his head. "Just one of the kids in the refugee camp. But this pic...it gets me, every time."

"I can see why," Emily said, removing her hand. And, for that moment, her trust. Because she seriously doubted the child had been *just* some kid in the camp. Then again, it wasn't as if Colin was under any obligation to rip open his soul to her. Especially if that soul, like hers, had been recently wounded.

A second later he shut the tiny laptop and stood to set it back on the desk, his hunched shoulders twisting Emily up inside.

"Are those going into your book?" she asked after what felt like an appropriate lapse.

"Some of them." Colin turned, looking very much like a man asking for understanding. Although—again—why from her, she had no idea. And for what, exactly, she had even less. "The publisher's going to donate a portion of the profits to The Little Ones' Rescue Fund."

"Put me down for ten copies," she said, and his grin at least somewhat unwound the tension.

"So..." She brought the tea to her lips again, only to make a face because it'd already gone cold. "How long ago was..." Her head tilted. "What was her name?"

"Oh," he said, as though surprised by her question. "Sarah. A year."

Emily got to her feet, shaking out her achy legs as she went to the kitchen to nuke her tea. "And you're still not over her, are you?"

Colin imagined she could probably feel him staring a hole between her shoulder blades as she set the mug inside a very early-generation microwave, punched in thirty seconds. When he didn't answer her, though, she turned, the microwave whirring behind her. "Sorry. Didn't mean to overstep—"

"No, it's not that, it's…"

Uh-huh. Answer that one, big shot.

Frowning, he cupped the back of his head for a moment, then shifted to lean back against the edge of the coffee table, one wrist propped on his raised knee as he let himself sink into those sweet, kind eyes. But he sensed a steeliness behind the sweetness a smart man would heed. Although how smart he actually was, was open to interpretation.

Colin looked down at the pup, passed out by his hip, curled up so tight he looked like a little potato. "I think…" He lifted his gaze to hers again—bracing himself against that damned tug of longing. "I think it's more that I wanted to believe she'd eventually see things my way. That somehow we'd work it out. My mistake was…" He stroked the dog, who groaned in his sleep. "In not realizing she was thinking exactly the same thing. So basically we wasted a couple years of our lives hoping the other person would change." A breath left his lungs. "Dumb."

The microwave dinged, after a fashion. Emily retrieved her tea and returned to the living room, then kicked off her flats to settle into Dad's old beat-up recliner, her feet underneath her, her hair rippling over her shoulders. Across her breasts. "Because you believed she was worth waiting for."

Not what he'd expected. Although what that might have been, he had no clue. Still, he pushed out a short laugh. "Sarah was—is—a great person. Funny, smart, gracious—all the boxes ticked. Except the biggie. Well, two biggies."

"And what's the second?"

Colin went very still for a moment, a little surprised to realize how weird it felt to talk about the woman who'd once taken up so much space in his head. His world.

"Kids," he said on a breath. "As in, she wanted them. After everything I'd seen… I wasn't so sure." He paused, waiting out the wave. "I'm still not."

It'd taken him a long time to fully admit that to himself. Let alone anyone else. Especially considering how genuinely crazy he was about children. But that was the problem, wasn't it?

"For way too long," he said, "I'd let feelings blind me to logic. To the truth, of who we both were. What we both wanted. Or didn't. A huge mistake I'm only grateful we realized before things got worse."

And wasn't that a careful expression on Emily's face? Then again, she'd hardly be the first woman to be repelled by a man saying he didn't want to be a father. But then she said, with a shrug, "Not everyone's cut out to be a parent. Different strokes and all that."

Of course, his reasons for not wanting children were more complicated than he was about to share with someone who was still more or less a stranger. Sure, he'd learned the hard way that without honesty, no relationship had a snowball's chance in hell of succeeding. But this wasn't a relationship. Nor would it become one, for many reasons. In which case he was under no obligation to give this woman total access to what lurked inside his skull.

Never mind that he'd already given her more of a glimpse than he'd intended.

So Colin picked up his own tea again and lobbed the conversation back to her.

"What about you? You want kids?"

On a half laugh, Emily cupped the mug to her chest, frowning into it. "Yes, but…" On a gusty sigh, she met his gaze again. "That was part of the fantasy, you know?"

"The fantasy?"

Emily nodded, then set the mug on the table beside

the chair before somehow rearranging her limbs to prop one elbow on her knee and rest her chin in her palm, a frown pinching her forehead. "Between the engagement and the wedding planning and everything…looking back, I have to wonder how much of that, really, was me playing *my* part in what my parents wanted for me." Another dry laugh preceded, "Okay, what I'd convinced myself I wanted, too. Because nobody forced me into this engagement, believe me. But…"

Shifting again, Emily set the mug on the side table to sit cross-legged, then leaned forward with her hands clasped in front of her. "I used to pore over my parents' wedding album for hours, absolutely fascinated with the whole… spectacle. *Lavish* doesn't even begin to cover it. The flowers, the crystal, the doves…the Carolina Herrera wedding gown. Which looked like sparkling whipped cream. Cannot tell you how much I drooled over that thing. Although my taste changed—blessedly—my jonesing for the dream wedding did not. The dream…life. You wanna talk *dumb*." Straightening, she jerked both thumbs toward her chest. "This girl, right here."

"Daddy's princess?"

Another snort preceded, "The definition of, believe me. Which is why…" Her mouth twisted to one side. "Even aside from the obvious, it's probably a blessing, the way things worked out. Or didn't. Because I obviously wasn't going into it with my eyes wide open. Or as a complete person, who knew what she needed. Wanted. *Deserved*. And I'm not talking about doves and a ten-thousand-dollar wedding gown."

Colin's brows slammed together. "Your gown really cost that much?"

"It really did. However…over the past few weeks I've realized I really, really missed the point. If not the boat.

Yes, I want kids. And to be a wife. But I wasn't as *ready* to be a wife and mother as I'd wanted to believe. Because I had gotten caught up in the fantasy. In everyone's expectations. Which in turn blinded me to the simple, if highly embarrassing, fact that I still had some growing up to do."

He hesitated, then said, "How old are you, anyway?"

She smirked. "Twenty-seven in two months. So not a child. Even if—" She stretched her arms up, arching her back, before letting them drop again. "Even if I often still feel like one."

Colin averted his gaze from her breasts. "Because you ran away from home."

Her eyes crinkled. "Says the man who did the same thing *how* many years ago? And hadn't been back in years?"

Touché.

Colin scooped up the dog and got to his feet, depositing the pup in Emily's lap before taking his empty cup to the kitchen to rinse it out. "You hungry? I've got popcorn—"

"No, thanks. I'm good. So you know why I escaped. Your turn."

"And there's such a thing as taking this forthrightness thing too far."

"It's not exactly a secret, Colin. That you left, I mean. Why, however—"

"And my brother didn't fill you in?"

"Actually, I don't think he really knows. Or if he does, he's not saying. Fraternal honor, or something."

Of course, Josh had been a teenager when Colin bolted from the nest like his tail feathers were on fire. And it wasn't as if Colin had talked things over with any of his brothers, not even Zach. Still, speaking of things not exactly being secret...

"I felt like I was about to suffocate here," he said, shoving a popcorn packet into the microwave and hoping for the best. "What you said, about expectations?" He turned back to see she'd twisted around in the chair to watch him, the puppy nestled in that sweet spot between the tops of her breasts and her chin. Hell. He almost had to literally shake his head loose from his ass. "The family's been here for generations, working cattle and horses on the Vista. We are all on horses by three or four, rounding up cattle by six. So it was assumed that Zach and I, especially, would follow family tradition in one way or another. And when Zach announced he wanted to become a vet, Dad naturally assumed the ranch foreman mantle would fall to me."

Emily frowned. "Without bothering to find out if that's what you wanted to do?"

"There was never even a question in his mind. Only around the time I hit puberty, I realized I felt like I was choking. And not only from the dust kicked up by a hundred head of cattle deciding they didn't want to go where you wanted 'em to. The funny thing is, we traveled a lot when my brothers and I were kids—there were enough hands to fill in so we could do that—because my folks insisted we see there was a world beyond this little corner of New Mexico. What they didn't realize, however, was that those road trips only whetted my appetite for more. I may not have known what that *more* was, at that point, but I sure as heck knew I'd never find it if I didn't leave. And Dad and I didn't exactly see eye to eye on that."

"Because this *was* his world."

"Exactly. And he couldn't, or wouldn't, see my side of things. Said I'd never be happy looking for something 'out there' if I didn't find it right where I was first."

Emily looked down at the puppy for a moment. "Not an unreasonable point."

"On the surface? No. Even if at the time I thought he

was off his nut. Because all I could think was that I'd die if I had to live out the rest of my life within twenty miles of where I'd been born."

"And I take it you still feel that way," Emily said behind him when he turned to get the scorched popcorn out of the microwave, dumping the mess in the garbage.

Colin shoved open the window over the sink to air out the place—not to mention his head—before facing her again, his arms crossed over his chest. Gal had enough of her own crap to sort through without him dragging up his own conflicts. "I wanted to make a difference," he said at last, deciding keeping things in the past tense was safer, for the moment at least, than messing around in the present. "In the world, I mean. And I couldn't do that here. Not like I wanted to, anyway." Then he pushed a short laugh through his nose. "Although all these years later, it's not like I'm a doctor or anything. I'm not exactly saving lives—"

"And don't you dare sell yourself short," Emily said, almost vehemently. "There's a lot to be said for simply bearing witness to what's going on in the world, shining a light on all the stuff a lot of people don't know about. Or don't *want* to know about. Maybe you're not healing bodies, but…but if your work shakes some people out of their complacency, heals a few souls in the process…" Her cheeks flushed as her mouth clamped shut. Then she shoved out a breath. "We all have our place in the world. If that's yours, just own it, dude." Then she pushed out a tired laugh. "Listen to me, sounding like some expert."

One side of Colin's mouth pushed up. "You ask me, most of those *experts* spend way too much time talking out of their butts. And you look like you're about to topple over."

A short laugh collided with her yawn. "I guess I am.

Well, puppydoodle," she said, pushing herself upright with the pup still nestled under her chin, "guess I better turn you over to Uncle Colin." Naturally the dog swung around to gnaw on the ends of her hair, making her laugh… And her scent, and that damned laugh, drifted up to Colin, surrounding him like a hug.

He didn't want her to leave. Meaning he desperately needed her to do exactly that.

Especially when they got to his door and she looked up at him, a half smile teasing that full mouth, and said, "Sometimes, all you can do is trust that things will work out exactly the way they're supposed to."

Colin crossed his arms, in no small part to keep from touching her. "Meaning?"

"That's where the trust part of that comes in," she said softly, then left, taking her scent and her laughter and a good chunk of Colin's good sense with her. He watched her until she disappeared, then shut the door and set the pup back down on the rug. With a shudder of pure joy, the tiny thing belly-crawled over to the rope toy Emily had bought for him and started to gnaw on it, blissfully unaware of the storm raging inside Colin's head. Because *damn it*—who the hell's bright idea was it, anyway, plopping this woman in front of him? It was downright cruel, the way the light shined from inside her as steady as a little lighthouse grounded on solid rock, impervious to the crashing waves determined to take it under.

Granted, maybe her situation didn't even begin to compare with the horrors he'd witnessed. And by her own admission, she'd fled from "real" life to give herself space to heal. Kinda hard to fault her for that, though, since wasn't he doing the same thing? Even so, what he'd seen in her eyes when she looked at those photos—even without knowing the whole story—punched Colin in the gut almost as bad as the subjects had to begin with. However much her own heart might still be shredded, it still overflowed with compassion for others…the hallmark of somebody made of far sterner stuff than she probably even realized. And damned if that hadn't put *his* heart in danger.

In other words, Emily wasn't the only one being assaulted by some big-ass waves.

Colin could only pray for the strength to withstand the ones crashing over him half as well as the woman who'd just caused the tsunami.

Chapter Seven

"I think you've got customers," Emily whispered to Dee, who was helping Jesse Aragon, a young Native artist she was promoting, hang one of his in-your-face paintings of the nearby mountains on the deliberately neutral wall. Dee had decided the smartest thing was to set up the gallery as a co-op for now, the artists themselves pitching in with their labor and time to help run the place until it was in the black.

Although judging from the pair of tourists currently peering and pointing through the large plate glass window, that wasn't going to take long.

In a floaty-print top and dusty capris, Dee crossed to the door to let them in, even though the official opening wasn't for another week yet. And in they swooped, along with the lilac-scented May breeze.

"Are you even open?" a middle-aged, much-too-tan man asked, his eyes hungrily darting around the gallery, and Emily smiled. Ninety percent of them were looky-loos, more curious than serious. But this one—and his wife, her wrists and chest choked with heavy silver-and-turquoise Navajo jewelry—were so obviously collectors it was almost amusing.

"Close enough," Dee said with a big grin, shoving a hand through her freshly cropped hair. "As long as you don't mind a little dirt." From the portacrib set up apart from the chaos, baby Katie let out a squawk. Dee laughed. "Or kids."

"Oh…" The woman made a beeline for the baby, who gave her new admirer her brightest, most adorable grin. "Isn't she precious! Is she yours?"

Chuckling, Dee joined the woman to haul Katie up into her arms, while her husband and the artist immediately slipped into a deep conversation about the painting…which the guy had apparently fallen immediately in love with. Dee glanced over at Emily, her eyes sparkling even more than the tiny diamond in her nose. Her cousin had reverted to the edgy look from her DC gallery days—a costume, yes, but at least one Dee knew she was wearing. And why.

A thought that led Emily to thinking about Colin. Again. In fact, she'd come into town with Dee today partly to distract herself from exactly that, even though she hadn't seen Josh's brother in the week or so since he'd taken the puppy. Because something told her Colin was also wearing a costume, of sorts, even if his was entirely mental. Granted, after Michael, her Spidey senses were probably on overdrive, but…

And did she need such folderol in her life? She did not. Bad enough she'd already fallen in love with a *dog* that would never be hers.

Especially since she knew—*knew*—that objectivity probably wasn't her strong suit right now. Maybe her wounds weren't open and raw and bleeding, but even she knew she was still too bruised and tender to think straight. Because who was in classic rebound mode right now, yearning for affirmation that she was desirable? Uh-huh. Meaning the way Colin looked at her that night had gotten all sorts of juices going, as one would expect when said juices had been neglected—if not outright ignored—for more than a year.

Her cell phone chirped at her. Not her mother, at least, whom she'd finally talked to a few days ago. Because a pleaser doesn't simply flip a switch and become *that* daughter. Alas. But it had been a strained—and strange—conversation, one that God willing wouldn't be reprised anytime soon.

Although seeing her father's number on the display didn't exactly fill Emily with glee, either, since Stewart Weber and she had never really had much to say to each other. Her father had been perfectly content to stay out of his wife's way, letting Margaret steer the family ship as she saw fit. Emily supposed her father loved her, in his own detached way. Even if he'd often looked at her as though not quite sure how he'd come to have a daughter. So his calling her now...

She braced herself.

"That you, Emily?"

Figuring she probably didn't want witnesses for this conversation, she stepped out of the gallery to sit on a wrought iron bench in front, where the warm sun convinced her to unbutton her cardigan. "Nobody else is going to be answering my phone, Dad."

"Oh. Of course." She imagined him blinking behind his steel-rimmed glasses, tugging on the bow tie he was never without, even when he was hermited in his study, researching or writing. Hiding out from his wife, most likely. Although he'd had other "outlets," too, hadn't he? Outlets Emily hadn't known about until she was in high school. "So. How are you?"

"I'm fine. Which I'm sure Mom told you."

"And maybe I wanted to hear it for myself and not through your mother's filter."

Whoa. Had he actually snapped at her? She'd never known her father to lose his cool with anyone. Not even with her mother, who, heaven knew, provided the man with ample opportunity for losing it. Not to mention an excuse, she supposed, for his behavior.

"What's going on, Dad?"

"You need to come home, that's what's going on."

Home. Yes, she'd told Colin she'd probably go back. Because that was logical. Practical. Because she had no reason, really, to stay here. Except what was *there* for her now? Really?

"Why?"

"Your mother's about to drive me crazy. She's in here every five minutes, either in tears or yelling or both. I can't get a damn thing done for all the interrupting. The…emotions exploding all over everything…" No, he'd never liked those very much, had he? "I know she's worried about you, but she's taking it out on me. And that's not right."

Anger—which wasn't exactly in short supply these days—surged through Emily's chest, heat racing up her neck, across her cheeks. "And you know what? *I'm* the one who had the rug yanked out from under her, the one who was humiliated. The one who was *cheated on.*" Okay, so she might've put the screws in a bit with that one. "So I'm sorry if Mother's taking her frustration out on you that *her* plans got screwed up, but right now, I need to take care of myself. Figure out what *I* need to do. To *be.* Meaning it's up to you guys to figure out how to deal with each other.

Or not. Go complain to one of your mistresses, Dad. Or is that not part of their job description?"

Her father's silence actually rang in her ear.

"What did you say?"

She pushed out a harsh laugh. "You honestly think I didn't know? That I haven't been playing the same game the two of you were, pretending everything was fine when it wasn't? Being the good, obedient daughter because it kept peace in the house. Or maybe that's only what I wanted to believe, that if I somehow tried a little harder I could fix whatever was broken between you. That I could..." She swatted at a tear that had escaped out of the corner of her eye. "That I could somehow make us into something that at least *looked* like a real family."

In the wake of her father's silence, she scrubbed the space between her brows. "Which I suppose made me exactly like Mother, didn't it? Who's only ever cared about appearances. Which is why she's got her panties in such a twist now, because *her* dream wedding for her daughter went up in smoke. Yes, I'll own my role in going along with it all, which is part of what I'm dealing with now. I wasn't a totally innocent bystander. Still. Whatever your issues are with Mother, I can't be your buffer anymore. Because you know what? If I'm here trying to figure out how to handle my own life, I think it's way past time the two of you figured out yours. Stay together or don't, I don't care. But for heaven's sake, be freaking *honest* with each other. Not to mention with yourselves."

Another long spate of silence preceded, "That's no way for a child to speak to her parent."

"Yeah, well, maybe that's because I'm not a child anymore."

Shaking, she cut off the call...

…only to look up to see Colin standing a few feet away, his expression unreadable behind his sunglasses.

Guessing by the deep blush that blazed across her cheeks, Emily really hadn't known he was there. Not that Colin had tried to sneak up on her or anything—as big as he was, that would've been impossible, anyway—but apparently she'd been too engrossed in her conversation to notice much of anything.

And by the time he realized exactly how personal the call was, it was too late for any kind of a graceful exit. Meaning he couldn't decide whether to feel like a jerk… or proud as hell of her.

"Sorry," he said, grateful they were alone, at least. Things would get busier later on, once school let out and the summer tourists descended, but this time of year what passed for downtown Whispering Pines vacillated between slow and dead.

"It's okay," Emily said, her eyes closing as she let her head drop back against the adobe wall behind the bench. Although the frown etched into her forehead said otherwise. "How much did you hear?"

"Probably more than you want to know." Eyes still closed, she grunted. "That can't have been easy."

After a moment, she opened her eyes, then patted the space beside her on the bench. Colin hesitated, then sat. And of course a breeze picked that exact moment to blow her scent in his direction. Whatever it was, it should be illegal. Especially since, even after a week, he could still smell her in his house. Although he'd be willing to bet that was the power of suggestion.

She forked her fingers through her ponytail, which cascaded over one breast like a caramel-colored waterfall, and

Colin had to look away. "At least you had the courage to leave before things got toxic," she said.

Feeling his own face warm, Colin leaned forward, his hands linked between his spread knees. "I don't know that I would've put it that way back then, but…maybe." His mouth pushed to one side. "Levi was the one who seemed to actually get off on getting up in Dad's face about stuff. Whereas I…"

"Escaped?"

"Pretty much." He hauled in a breath. "It's hard to stand up for yourself when you haven't figured out yet who you are."

Emily released a soft laugh. "Tell me about it."

His gaze swung to the side of her face. "So I take it you just did?"

That got another, stronger laugh. "I wish. I mean…" Her brow pleated, she faced him again. "I think I'm finally getting a feel for what I *need* to do. To *be*." She looked away again. "But right now, it's like…a glimmer. A promise. I've got a ways to go before I get any real handle on who I am, you're right. That conversation…it was a first tiny step on the beginning of a long, very overdue journey. One I have to take by myself."

In other words, she was right where Colin had been all those years ago, when everything was so new and shiny, if a little scary. In some ways he almost envied her.

He also hadn't missed the "by myself" part of all of that.

She was absolutely right, of course. Trying to figure out all the stuff she clearly needed to figure out would be nearly impossible with another person tossed into the equation. And her *recognizing* that was admirable as hell. Never mind the small, selfish, extraordinarily stupid part of him that actually had the nerve to feel disappointed. What the hell?

Half smiling, Colin leaned back again, his arms folded high on his chest. "No, I'd say the *first* step was you coming out here. Breaking away. But what I just heard… I'd say that was a much bigger step than you're giving yourself credit for."

"Thanks," she said after a moment. "Although I can't hide forever. Much as I might like to. A little space to get my head on straight is all well and good, but even I know I need to face my issues with my parents head-on. Otherwise I'm simply doing what I've always done." Her mouth pulled flat. "And sooner rather than later, before I totally wear out my welcome. But not until after the wedding, I imagine."

Colin watched as a young couple he didn't recognize walked hand in hand across the street, window-shopping. "That's next week." A realization that hit him way harder than it should've, that she'd be leaving soon. After all, wouldn't that make his own decision easier?

"Ten days. And I know. My parents don't, though. That I'm staying until then."

"Rebel," he said, and she laughed. A nice laugh, low and rich. One he wouldn't mind hearing closer to his ear…

"So what're you doing in town, anyway?" she asked.

"Needed to get out for a minute," Colin said, jerking his thoughts back in line. "Get away. Like I said before. And Josh'd said something about Deanna being almost ready to open the gallery, so I thought I'd kill a couple birds with one stone and come see." He twisted around to look inside through the plate glass window. "She's already got customers?"

Emily chuckled, then got to her feet. "Heck, she's already sold three pieces, and arranged a commission on a fourth. Not that I'm surprised," she said, facing the wide window with a grin stretched across her face. "I never doubted for a minute Dee could make a go of this. She's got an eye like none other. Not to mention business smarts that'd put most CEOs to shame."

And damned if her obvious pride in her cousin didn't provoke an ache so sharp it actually hurt. Ignoring it— sorta—Colin stood as well, his hands jammed in his front pockets. "Deanna's real lucky to have a friend like you."

Emily twisted around, her smile somehow reaching inside Colin to twist him up even harder. "Dee's been a good friend to me, too. Even when I didn't deserve it. Well." She nodded toward the door. "Shall we?"

"Sure," Colin said, when all he really wanted to do was take his butt somewhere, anywhere, where Emily wasn't. Where he couldn't see the sun teasing those silky golden strands tangling with her eyelashes or hear that laugh or *smell* her, God help him.

Someplace where that combination of bone-deep goodness and rebelliousness couldn't slap him around until he didn't know which end was up…even as it reminded him of someone else who'd had that exact same effect on him.

And look how that had worked out. Or hadn't.

However, he supposed he could tough it out for another couple of weeks, if he had to, until she left, went back to her real life. Another couple of weeks to ignore the ache and the pull and all the rest of it.

He could do that, sure. Piece of cake.

The next morning, Emily came out to the kitchen to see her cousin seated at the table rocking a wailing, red-cheeked Katie, Mama looking pretty much like she was an inch away from tears herself. On his knees in a chair beside her and fisting spoonfuls of Cocoa Puffs into his mouth like there was no tomorrow, Austin kept giving his baby stepsister the side-eye, as though wishing she'd shut up already.

"Another tooth coming in," Dee said over the caterwauling. She was still in her pajamas, her hair porcupined around her slightly gray face. "I'm supposed to take Austin into school this morning, but…"

Already dressed in jeans and a lightweight cardigan over her sleeveless shirt, Emily drew a cup of coffee from the pot on the counter and sat across from Dee, her heart turning over in her chest at the miserable duo in front of her. She knew how grateful Josh and Dee both were for the part-time preschool the town's sole elementary school had set up for kids headed for kindergarten the following year, not only to get Austin used to the classroom setting but to give all of them a little breathing room while baby Kate was being so fussy. And normally Josh would have taken the boy to school, since clearly Dee wasn't going to make it this morning. But he'd gone with Zach into Taos to check out a potential addition to his stable and wouldn't be back until later that morning.

"So I'll take him," Emily said with a grin for the little boy, who grinned back around a mouthful of mashed cereal. "And then when I return—" she turned her smile on her exhausted cousin "—I'm taking over the wee banshee so her mommy can get some sleep."

"Oh, I couldn't—"

"Dee? Shut. Up." She glanced over at a wide-eyed Austin. "And don't you dare repeat me or your mother may not ever let me talk to you again."

Deanna pushed out a tired laugh. "You kidding? At this rate I may never let you leave."

A thought that provoked all manner of ambivalence inside Emily's already overwrought brain. Especially since, truth be told, she hadn't been getting a whole lot of sleep, either, these past few nights. Add to that her conversation yesterday with the reason behind her sleepless nights and…uh, boy. Although even she knew the chat itself had far less to do with her insomnia than what hadn't been said. And most likely wouldn't be. But man, oh, man—being around Colin was like walking under a power line in a thunderstorm. *Zzzzt!*

Because everything she'd said, about needing space to figure out who she was and what she wanted, was true. She didn't dare let herself get sucked into another relationship. Certainly not anytime soon. And *especially* not with someone who sent those Spidey senses off the charts, man. But the way he looked at her…

"What time's school start?" Emily said, carrying her empty mug to the sink, as if she could walk away from all the stuff going on inside her head. Stuff that could oh-so-easily lead to wrapping the man up in her arms and…

Yeah. *And.*

Such an innocent little word, so rife with the potential for disaster.

Emily rinsed out the mug, thinking it wouldn't hurt to give the kitchen another once-over. Not to mention get on her cousin's case about finally letting a cleaning service come in every once in a while. Especially now that the gallery was about to open for real.

"Nine," Dee said behind her. "And take my car, since the booster seat's already in it. I can go into town later."

Emily turned, glaring at her cousin as she swiped a towel inside the mug. "After you've had a nap."

Dee's mouth twisted. "Yes, Mother."

"You ready, munchkin?" she said to Austin, who gave a vigorous nod and more or less fell out of his chair, rolling his eyes when Dee reminded him to go pee before he got in the car. A moment later, he roared to the back door, emitting something like a battle cry. Although you could barely hear it over the baby's screams.

The volume stayed full blast as they wended through sun-drenched ranchland and peaceful forest on their way to town, Austin singing gustily behind her. The weird thing was, even though she'd been an only child in a house that redefined *hushed*, the noise and general craziness of her cousin's house didn't bother her. Because at least that was *real*.

Children of all ages swarmed the entrance to the small brick school building, predominantely black-haired heads gleaming in the sun, the local population being more Native or Hispanic than gringo. Austin's teacher, too, wore a long, dark braid that trailed between her widely set shoulder blades, her wrists and fingers adorned with turquoise-and-silver jewelry Emily was guessing had been in her family for a while.

"This is Emily!" Austin announced, his little chest puffed out, which in turn sparked something lovely and warm inside Emily's.

"Deanna's cousin," she said, shaking the teacher's hand. The young woman's smile was almost blindingly bright against skin not dissimilar in tone to the reddish-brown tones so prevalent in the landscape…as befitted the Natives' spiritual ties to Mother Earth.

"Susana Ortiz," she said, smiling, then cupped Austin's curls. "Go on inside, cutie. Have a seat in the reading circle."

Glancing inside the classroom, chock full of little kids, Emily frowned. "I thought Dee said there were only ten kids in his class."

Susana sighed. "Normally, yes. But our pregnant kindergarten teacher is now on bed rest until she delivers. So we're down one until we get a sub. Which isn't that easy out here in the sticks, as I'm sure you can imagine. I hope we find someone soon, though. Twenty-five little kids is a lot to handle, even with a teacher's aide. At least, to handle well. Give them the individual attention they deserve. And *need*, especially when they're on such different tracks. At least it's only for a few weeks, until school lets out. I only hope they find someone for next year while she's on maternity leave… What?"

Emily had had no idea what seeing all those little kids together would do to her head, not to mention her heart. But surely she couldn't…

Could she?

And what's stopping you, missy?

She met the teacher's curious gaze again. "I'm accredited in Maryland and Virginia, to teach kindergarten and early childhood. I'd be happy to help out, if you need it—"

"Are you kidding?" Susana's dark eyes glittered. "If you're already certified… We'd have to rush through a background check, but…oh, my goodness. Are you sure? I mean, that would be such a blessing, I can't tell you!"

"Then whatever you need, I'm good." Emily looked back into the classroom, where Susana's assistant was doing a passable job of corralling enough energy to light up a small city.

A small girl-person attached herself to her teacher, tugging her back into the classroom. "Stop by the office," Susana said before the horde swallowed her up, "talk to the principal. We'll take it from there…"

Forty-five minutes later, Emily rushed back inside her cousin's house, apologizing profusely before she'd even found Dee calmly nursing little Katie in a pool of sunshine in the great room.

"It's okay," the brunette whispered, smiling down at her daughter, then back at Emily. "She calmed down right after you left, and it's been totally copacetic since. We both even passed out for a while. So what's going on?"

Emily had texted her, of course, to tell her she'd be a little late, so she wouldn't worry. But she hadn't said why, hadn't wanted to until she knew it was a done deal. Now she sat on the chair across from Dee, her heart pounding a mile a minute as Smoky jumped up on her lap, *mwwrowing* for attention.

"I think I just talked my way into a job," she said, laughing, and her cousin's eyes went wide as dinner plates.

Chapter Eight

The midday sun beating down on his shoulders and uncovered head, Colin snapped photo after photo of his soon-to-be sister-in-law seated in her special saddle as she calmly instructed the young boy on the palomino a few feet away on the other side of the corral fence. Even though he couldn't use the pics without the boy's parents' permission, it felt good, getting back into the swing of things. Shoot, before this morning he hadn't even taken any landscape shots, and that was a crying shame.

But something—maybe seeing the artwork up in Deanna's gallery the day before, maybe simply being here—had prodded his muse awake at the crack of dawn to catch the sunrise drenching the mountains in shades of violet and rose, gilding the pastures and barns, even the horses his brother had already let out to graze. He wouldn't publish those, either—hell, everybody and his cousin took sunrise pictures, for God's sake—but he hadn't realized until today exactly how much he'd missed this crucial part of who he was.

Off in another paddock, Josh worked a young horse, training him to cut cattle from a small, young herd here on a short-term arrangement for that very purpose. The place was definitely quieter now than when he'd been a kid, on those early mornings when cutting calves from their mamas for branding and deworming had resulted in a whole lot of mournful lowing, human as well as bovine. Add to that a bunch of cowboys yelling and dogs barking, the whoops of victory when a particularly ornery calf finally cooperated…the enormous breakfasts his mother and Gus, the Vista's old housekeeper, had provided when the morning's work was done…

Colin lowered the camera, his forehead puckered. No, maybe he'd wanted more than that life. But thinking back on it now, even the parts he'd been so sure he hated hadn't been all bad, had they? In fact, watching Josh working that horse, the animal's beauty and grace and intelligence as it darted and danced in the dust at his rider's cues, cutting calf after calf from the fidgety clot on one side of the corral, brought to mind a whole lot of pleasant memories.

As did watching Mallory calmly encouraging the boy on the sweet, patient horse—

Footsteps in the dirt behind him made him turn, his heart knocking as he watched Emily striding toward him, looking far more like a country gal in her jeans and sleeveless shirt than she had any right to. Especially with her hair pulled off her face into a single braid trailing down her back. She was even wearing cowboy boots. Deanna's, he was guessing, by how beat-up they were.

Wordlessly, she came up beside him, her hands shoved in the back pockets of a pair of jeans that might as well have been painted on her. He'd seen her pull up to the main house in Dee's truck a little bit ago, had wondered where she'd gone. Now he noticed she was practically crackling with energy, wearing a grin that was doing very bad things to his head. Among other things.

"Whatcha doing?"

He held up the camera. "Getting back in the groove. You?"

"Actually…" The grin flashed again. "I might have a job."

A weird little *ping* went off in his midsection. "A job? Here?"

"Yes, *here*. Although it's not definite yet." She tilted her head, probably in response to his horrified expression. "Is this a problem?"

Colin turned away. "No, of course not." He took another shot. "Doing what?"

"Herding small children, aka teaching. They're short a teacher at Austin's school, so I might fill in for the rest of the year. If I pass the background check, that is."

"Any reason why you wouldn't?"

Her laugh brought his gaze back to hers. "I might've thought nefarious things about my ex, but since I didn't carry any of them out…" She shrugged. "I think I'm good." Damn. She was positively glowing, no other word for it. "But seriously, it's as if an angel dropped the perfect thing right into my lap, you know? And right here in itty-bitty Whispering Pines. Crazy."

"Although it's temporary, you said?"

"Well, there's a possibility of it becoming full-time next year, but… I don't know. I can't really think that far into the future at this point. For now, though, it's perfect. Because *kids*," she said, releasing a blissful sigh. "Since getting to teach is the next best thing to being a mama myself one day. Although…" She made a face. "Heaven knows when that might happen. I suppose I could adopt as a single mom, though. Right? Which might be a more viable alternative than waiting for the—" she made air quotes "—*right guy* to come along. For me, anyway. Since my judgment clearly sucks."

Colin fiddled with the aperture on the lens to get another shot of the kid. In other words, her life was every bit as unsettled as his. If not more. At least he had something to go back to, something he was good at, that defined him. Clearly Emily didn't have a clue. Nor should she right now, not after what she'd just been through.

"And maybe you shouldn't be so hard on yourself."

She shrugged again, unconcerned. "At least it's an excuse to pig out on junk food, so there's that. Although since I'm like a brownie away from not being able to button my jeans anymore, that particular indulgence is about to come to a screeching halt."

He had to smile. "You think your folks will be okay with this new development?"

"Since it's my life, what can they say? God, it's a gorgeous day," she said, twisting around to rest her elbows on the fence's top rail, lifting her makeup-free face to the sun. The way the light angled across her nose, her lips…he itched to take her photo so badly he practically hummed with it, but he had no idea how to do that without coming across as weird. Or lame. Or both.

"Hope you're wearing sunscreen," he said, looking away.

That got another throaty laugh before she heaved herself up onto the top rail, hooking the heels of her boots on top of the one below. "Not my first time out here, remember? I know all about the high altitude." Her hands clamped on to the rail on either side of her hips, she twisted to watch Mallory with the boy. "You know about the kid?"

"Not really, no."

"He's the son of some friends of Mallory's from back in LA. They're staying up at the resort, ran into her and Zach in town. Josh said the kid's got some sort of developmental issues, although he's not sure what they are. But Mallory apparently told them about her facility—with the idea that when she was fully up and running, they might consider sending the boy there. Only they immediately asked if she'd work with him a little while they were here. And being Mallory, she said yes. That's her son's horse," she said, nodding toward the beautiful animal, his coat glistening in the sun. Then she humphed a short laugh. "Waffles."

"Pardon?"

"The horse's name. Waffles."

Colin smiled. "There were some crazy names when I was a kid, too. For years, I rode one named Ebenezer."

"As in Scrooge?"

"Yep. Have no idea who named him that. Or why. I took to calling him Jack, though. He didn't seem to care."

Emily crossed her arms. Wobbled. Colin instinctively clamped a hand on her thigh to steady her, heat shooting through him when she covered his hand with hers, her other one grabbing the edge of the fence rail again.

"Got it, thanks, I'm good," she said, and he removed his hand. Could still feel her, though. As in, his palm down-right tingled. Among other things. "Was he your buddy?"

"He was. And not only mine. Every so often Deanna's folks would invite groups of kids from as far away as Albuquerque to come to the ranch, to ride and learn how to work cattle, stuff like that." He felt another smile push at his mouth. "Jack was such a ham bone, I swear. He totally ate up the attention. And some of that attention was pretty intense, believe me. There were other kids, though…" A huge breath left his lungs as the memories came roaring back. "A lot of the kids came from not-so-great situations. Some were foster kids, removed from their homes because they'd been neglected. Or worse. Those kids…"

He met Emily's gaze again, his heart fisting at the look in her eyes. "The resentment, the fear and anger, just poured off 'em. Some wouldn't even talk. But Jack was so patient with them, like he knew they needed him to be more than a horse. And the kids…they knew Jack wouldn't judge them, or ask questions they couldn't answer, or even expect them to say anything. And by the end of those days, you'd be surprised how many of 'em…" He shook his head, then looked back out toward Mallory and the boy. "I'd like to think by the time they left, they felt a little better about life than they had when they got here."

"I'm sure," Emily said softly, and for a good two or three seconds his face warmed under her intense scrutiny. Then she glanced away. "Sounds like Jack was a good listener."

"He was. Especially for me, back when I needed to figure out a few things, too."

"Hmm." Emily was quiet for another several seconds before she said, "The other day when Mallory was here for lunch, she said something about how she could have never imagined five years ago—when the doctors told her she'd probably never walk again—how any good could have possibly come out of that. And yet her accident set off a series of events which led her back here, where she met Zach, who got her riding again when she'd convinced herself that would never happen. And now she's starting up this facility that maybe will help other people see beyond what the world sees as limitations."

Colin felt the muscles alongside his spine tense. "And your point is?"

"How differently people see things, I suppose. Places."
Her forehead pinched. "How Mallory saw promise and
potential and new beginnings in this little corner of the
world after seemingly losing everything—her career, her
first marriage. And I guess it's sort of the same for me, although heaven knows what I've been through doesn't even
begin to compare with her experience. Even so, I look at
all of this—" she waved one arm out to the sky "—and I
feel freer than I can ever remember. Like the possibilities
are as endless as the sky. And yet you…"

She lowered her arm to clutch the top of the rail again.
"You don't see it that way at all, do you?"

And damned if her question didn't arrow straight to the
very knot he was trying to unravel. "Life here felt very…
small." He hmmphed a short, dry laugh. "Which I suppose proves your point. That where you see all this endless possibility, I felt like I couldn't breathe."

"Almost exactly what Dee said, when she came to live
with us after Aunt Kathryn died. Huh."

"What?"

"I wonder…if it's not so much the where, or even the
what, but more of a need to break away from what we
know, what we're used to. That some people simply need
different in order to… I don't know. Feel complete, maybe?
As though they've explored *all* the possibilities. Others—
like Zach and Josh, your dad—don't. It's all about finding
our own place in the world, isn't it? Our purpose."

"Have you always been this philosophical?"

Her laugh warmed him. "Not hardly. Kinda hard to see
the bigger picture when you're busy trying to keep the
smaller one neatly framed. But it's true, isn't it? How we
go along, assuming we're on the right path, doing what
we're supposed to be doing, and then something happens
that forces us to rethink everything we thought was real…"

Another laugh burped from her chest. "I'm sorry, the thinner air is clearly wreaking havoc with my head. Feel free to ignore my ramblings. So…" She lowered herself to the ground again, dusting off her butt. "I guess next up is your brother's wedding?"

What she'd said about the air and her head? True. "Guess so."

For one crazy moment, he considered asking her to go with him. Because clearly she wasn't the only one dealing with the effects of the high altitude.

Except it was more than that, wasn't it? Because Emily Weber made him feel good. Made him *feel*, period. Not to mention, she listened. *Got* him, even, he thought. Hell, it was almost like being around old Jack again. Well, except for the fact he'd never been attracted to his horse.

And if he had a lick of sense he'd squelch his attraction to the woman standing beside him now. Just…swallow it down, bat it away, pretend he wasn't feeling what he was feeling.

"Any idea what's next?" she asked. "After the book's done?"

Perfectly logical question, considering what she knew about him. What he'd let her know, anyway.

"There's a couple of options." Which was true enough. "Haven't decided which one to go for, though." Also true. But honest to God—how was it he'd been a hundred times more sure at eighteen of what he at least *thought* he wanted than he was now?

She gave him one of those looks, like she could see straight through his BS. As unnerving as that was, it was also strangely comforting. Or might have been, if he hadn't been so thoroughly screwed up. "Options are good."

"They are. Absolutely."

Sympathy softened her gaze, made him want to lean in, see if—

"Guess you'll be glad to get away from here again."

"It hasn't been entirely horrible," he said quietly, by now nearly trembling with the urge to touch her. To somehow infect himself with her warmth and humor and resilience. Except how selfish, how unfair would that be? To both of them, but especially to her? She'd been through enough without his foisting Jerk 2.0 on her.

"Good to know," Emily said, smiling. "Well." She tapped the top of the fence rail, then started to back away. "If we don't run into each other before, guess I'll see you at the wedding. Give the pup a pat for me, okay?"

Then he watched her return to the house, the braid swishing against her back, thinking sometimes it was hell, being the good guy.

The wedding was a small affair, mostly family. Although, Emily mused as she tried to get Zach's toddler Liam to sit still long enough to clip on his bow tie, once you got all the family members together, *small* took on a whole other definition. And it had been tempting, too, to feel like an outsider, except for everyone's insistence that as Dee's cousin she was family by default.

Definitely light years apart from her own childhood, she thought as another toddler—a girl this time—raced through the bedroom in Mallory and Zach's house set aside for the children's prep space. Emily caught the dark-haired cutie, a bundle of giggles and tulle, and plopped her on the bed to put her shoes back on, her heart turning over when little Risa launched herself into Emily's arms to plant a great big squishy kiss on her cheek.

Her eyes stinging for reasons Emily didn't want to examine too hard, she hugged the little girl back, breathing in her sweet innocence and unfeigned optimism. She'd still been an infant, Emily knew, when her father had been killed while serving overseas…when Josh's brother Levi returned from his own service to make good on a promise he'd made to his best friend to look out for his wife and two young daughters. A promise that turned into nothing short of a blessing for all concerned.

Naturally, thinking about one Talbot brother led to thoughts of another she couldn't keep out of her mind, no matter what she did. Honestly, it'd taken everything she had in her, when he told her about his horse Jack and how he'd helped all those kids, not to point out it hadn't only been the *horse* who'd enjoyed the encounters so much. That for all Colin swore he'd felt hamstrung by life in the boonies, the way his face practically glowed when he shared those memories proved to Emily that clearly there'd at least been times where he'd felt a sense of purpose and fulfillment right here.

Of course, those experiences could've also been the seeds of what eventually pushed him out of the nest, to do more, *be* more…to be who he had to be.

Well. Once he left, he'd be out of her life for good, and that would be that.

This was nothing more than two people who happened to be in the same place for five minutes. And one of those people—as in, herself—was still smarting from some seriously raw battle scars. Even so, when Colin looked at her as though he wanted to suck God-knew-what out of her, somehow those scars didn't feel so prominent. Ugly. Permanent…

In a simple, floral-print sheath that emphasized her long, pretty neck, Deanna stuck her head into the bedroom, managing to look elegant and harried at the same time as she struggled to keep a wriggling infant in her arms. "Need help?" she said over the shrieks of several excited children.

Since corralling squirts was her forte, Emily had volunteered for short people duty so the family could get ready in relative peace…only to quickly realize there was a huge difference between handling kindergartners confined to a single room and a half dozen hyper kids already amped up on the many and varied goodies spread out on the picnic table on the deck out back.

The little girl disengaged from her neck, Emily swept a hank of loose hair off her cheek, only to relieve her cousin of baby Katie, kicking up a storm in her mother's arms. Squealing with delight, the baby settled onto Emily's lap to immediately grab her long necklace and stuff it into a very slobbery mouth. "You might want to check on the older boys, make sure shirttails are still tucked in, faces are clean, that sort of thing."

Her cousin laughed. "Since none of them are actually in the wedding party, Nanny Em, I'm gonna make an executive decision and say it's not worth the bother." Then she frowned. "You okay?"

"I just said—"

"Not talking about the kids," Dee said gently, coming into the room to sit beside Emily on the edge of the bed. "I mean the wedding."

Ironically, her own wedding to Michael would have been today, as well. Which only Dee knew, since she was supposed to have been Emily's maid of honor. Certainly Mallory and Zach hadn't when they finally settled on a date a few weeks ago.

"Don't be silly," Emily said, twisting Katie around to bounce her on her knee. "Of course I'm okay."

"Really?"

Her gaze swung to her cousin's. "Jeebus, Dee—are you *trying* to bum me out?"

"No. But I know you. Meaning I'm very acquainted with this annoying little habit you have of pretending you're all happy-happy when you're not."

Emily looked back at the baby to make a funny face at her, smiling when Katie giggled. "Which is better—" she buried her forehead in the baby's tummy, only to have to pry her hair out of a slimy fist "—than bringing everyone down with my own troubles. Right?"

"Except this is me, Em. And I'd hate to think I invited you out here to recover from what happened only to—"

"Only to what?" Emily said, swinging the baby back around on her lap to rest her cheek in her downy hair. "Unwittingly provide me with an opportunity to face a demon or six? To prove to myself I'm well and truly over Michael?"

Deanna rested her hand on Emily's back. "Are you?"

Emily huffed a breath. "Guess I'm about to find out, huh?"

"Oh, Em…"

"Okay, fine—watching you and Josh, and Levi with Val… Has it been hard, seeing you guys living the life I want? The life I thought I was going to *have*, up to a few weeks ago? Sometimes. Shoot, sometimes it's been hard to breathe, no lie. Envy can be a real bear. However…" Smiling, she shifted the chunky monkey on her lap to lay a hand on her cousin's wrist. "For one thing, I'm well aware of what you all went through before you got to this point. That your happy-ever-afters didn't simply fall in your laps. And knowing that makes me far more thrilled for you guys than sorry for myself. And for another…" She squeezed her cousin's wrist. "I refuse to let other people's joy make me miserable." At the tears welling in Dee's eyes, Emily tried a smile. "Seriously, how dumb is that? If anything it gives me hope. And anyway, since the job came through, you guys are stuck with me now, right?"

Pushing out a short laugh, Dee reached for her daughter, then leaned over to give Emily a one-armed hug. "That part, I'm not sorry about. And I guess we better get out there…"

"You go on. I probably need to fix my hair."

Her cousin glanced up and burbled another laugh. "You might want to, at that," she said, then left the room.

Sighing, Emily dug out a comb from her purse, then stood in front of the mirrored closet to undo her mangled 'do. A quick comb-through, a couple of twists and she was back in business, jabbing hairpins into it hard enough to scrape her scalp. The partially open bedroom window faced the back; she could hear voices, laughter. Joy. Tears threatened again. She blinked them back. Because she was happy. Thrilled, even, that at least one area of her life was falling into place.

Then her phone rang.

She was tempted to let her mother's call go to voice mail again, only to realize two things: one, of necessity this would be a short conversation, which worked to her advantage; and two, that she couldn't avoid the woman forever. Especially after the text she'd left her the day before about the job.

"Honestly, it's about time you answered the phone—"

"I know, Mother, I'm sorry. And unfortunately I can't stay on long now, either. Zach's wedding's about to start. You remember Zach? The oldest Talbot brother? Your niece's brother-in-law?"

She could practically hear the bristling. Meaning either the significance of the day hadn't occurred to her mother or she was being diplomatic enough not to mention it. Although Emily's bringing up Deanna hadn't exactly been diplomatic of her, she supposed. For reasons harking back to Dee's mother "marrying that damn cowboy" so many years before. And now…

"You can't be serious about staying out there."

"Why not?" The noise outside increased. "This is perfect for me, Mother. And I feel at home—"

"Your home is here, Emily Rose—"

"Sorry, I've got to go. Say hi to Dad for me."

If you two are talking, that is.

And yes, she heard the squawk as she disconnected the call. But honestly—all her life she'd done her mother's bidding. Gone to the schools her mother chose, took music lessons because her mother wanted her to, only hung out with friends her mother approved of. Nearly married her mother's choice for her.

"Well, no more," Emily muttered, checking her reflection in the mirror one last time before leaving the room. Because she was done being the good girl, doing what was expected of her in order to please someone *else*.

Meaning from now on, it was about her life, her choices. Her mistakes, if it came to that.

And she didn't think it was insignificant that the first person she saw when she got outside was Colin, his eyes finding hers like a pair of magnets.

Colin, who'd be leaving town sooner rather than later. Yep.

Now or never, a little voice whispered, and she shuddered all the way down to her freshly painted toenails.

"Throw it to me, Uncle Colin!"

"No, me!"

Chuckling, Colin lobbed the battered Frisbee toward Jeremy, Zach's oldest boy, laughing harder when somebody's hound dog intercepted the plastic disk and bounded off with it. Because, yes, this family brought dogs to their weddings. All pumping limbs and shrill yells, a small herd of kids raced after the coonhound as he led them on a merry chase around Zach and Mallory's park-like backyard, currently suffused with enough grill smoke to probably reach the Colorado border. Man, there were a lot of kids, between Zach's two and Austin, his brother Levi's two stepdaughters and Mallory's middle schooler, Landon. Chaos, in other words. Much like his own childhood, he thought as the tricolor hound brought back the Frisbee, the children hot on his heels.

Amazing, how quickly the family had grown in the past year. How much it would in all likelihood continue to expand, he thought, his gaze snagging on his sister-in-law Val's huge belly. Three weddings, there'd been in that short amount of time. None of them big, fancy affairs— Josh and Deanna, in fact, had gone the justice-of-the-peace route. But it was kind of hard to ignore the fact that Colin was now officially the only unmarried son.

And even harder to ignore how much that bothered him. Even though contemplating the alternative didn't exactly sit well, either.

He tugged the disk out of the dog's jaws, motioning for the kids to get back so he could toss it again. One of the older girls caught it before the dog did, doing a little victory dance before tossing it to Austin. But at the poke at his knee, Colin looked down to see a little redheaded elf grinning up at him. Liam, Zach's youngest. Without a moment's hesitation he hauled the preschooler up into his arms, even though he nearly choked on the bittersweetness that holding his youngest nephew close provoked. The memories, of another little boy, on the other side of the world—

The puppy—still with him, still nameless—waddled back to attack Colin's sneaker. Laughing, Liam wriggled out of Colin's arms to plop on the grass by the little mutt-sky, laughing even harder when he suddenly had a face full of excited doggy, trying to lick everywhere at once. Colin lowered himself to the ground, his heart lurching when Liam immediately snuggled into his lap as if he'd known his "new" uncle all his life, and Colin felt like he'd just won the lottery.

From the other side of the yard, he heard Emily's laugh as she chatted easily with his parents. More easily than he did, probably. When she'd come out of the house before the ceremony, and their gazes had caught…well, for a moment there he could have sworn there was something between them. Something real, that was. The kind of something you grabbed with everything you had in you and hung on to for dear life.

And clearly all that smoke was getting to him. Although, the way she was glowing…what was that all about? Not her job, he didn't think, since that wasn't exactly news anymore. And anyway, she'd said it was probably only temporary. Interesting, how they both got off on kids—

Colin closed his eyes against the stab, which he'd hoped would have dulled by now. And he supposed it had, a little. Not enough, though. Not nearly enough.

"Liam!" Jeremy called to his little brother, his hands cupped around his mouth. "Wanna play tag?"

"Yeah!" the kid yelled back, pushing up from Colin's lap and taking off toward his cousins, who'd commandeered a flattish patch of grass bordering a small orchard, the later bloomers still in full flower. The property, though still suffering some from more than twenty years of abandonment and neglect, was one of the prettiest he'd ever seen, edging closer to the forest than most in the area. Colin smiled—he somehow doubted that when Mallory bought the property in the fall she'd had any idea she'd be married right here less than a year later.

Colin heaved himself to his feet and returned to a weather-beaten picnic table set apart from the deck, underneath a lazily shivering cottonwood, whistling for the pup to follow. Zach had told him earlier he might've found a home for the mutt; Colin in turn told himself the news hadn't poked at a sore spot he hadn't even known was there. Yes, despite logically knowing he couldn't keep the dog, not with the kind of life he led. He parked himself on top of the table to watch the goings-on from a relatively— as it were—safe distance. Not that he'd be alone for long, he imagined, since it was inevitable that a brother or parent or kid would sidle over sooner or later to engage him in conversation. But for right now, this worked. For him, anyway.

Because all this copaceticness was a bit hard to take. Especially concentrated like this, all in one spot.

His own grumpiness irritating the hell out of him, Colin lifted his previously abandoned can of beer to his lips as the pup rustled around in the sparse grass underneath the table, hunting bugs or something. Josh's twin, Levi, was manning the grill, one arm draped around Val's shoulders, her hands cupped over her huge belly—another girl, his mother had said, due any minute. Over near the house Zach and his new bride were laughing at something Dad was saying. The setting sun seemed to envelop the couple, sizzling in Mallory's wild red hair, glinting off the rims of her wheelchair. Zach stood slightly behind her, one hand underneath all that hair, resting on her shoulder, protective and *there*. And despite his own bad mood, Colin had to smile at his brother's loopy grin when Mallory's hand reached up to rest on his…only to feel his gut torque when Zach leaned over to brush a kiss over his wife's mouth. And how stupid was that, being envious of his brother for finding a second shot at heaven after the hell he'd been through?

Soundly chiding himself, Colin looked away…only to feel his gut fist all over again when he noticed Emily coming toward him, a can of diet soda dangling from her long fingers, her lips curved in that Mona Lisa smile that drove him crazy. She was wearing a sleeveless, pale yellow dress that rippled around her calves as she walked, so plain it should have been boring. How she somehow made it anything but was a mystery.

How she'd somehow fused herself to his psyche in a few short weeks was even more of one. The absurdity, not to mention the impracticality, of that fusing aside.

"Hey," she said, then bent to let the puppy chew her fingers for a minute before picking him up to cuddle underneath her chin. She'd twisted her hair into some sort of sloppy bun, leaving a bunch of strands dangling over her shoulders like Spanish moss. The whole look was crazy sexy, although he doubted that'd been her intention.

Colin nodded, telling himself it was this whole lovey-dovey atmosphere making him want to tug her close, feel her softness. Her warmth. Hear that chuckle in his ear. Not loneliness. No, certainly not that. "Congratulations," he said, and she gave him a puzzled little grin.

"For what?"

"Surviving a Talbot family do."

She laughed. "Thanks. Although your congrats might be a bit premature. Since it's not over yet." Grinning, she waved the can at the table. "Mind if I join you?"

Oh, hell, yes. "Not at all."

Shifting the dog into the arm holding the soda, she

clutched a fistful of dress to hike it up to her knees, then climbed onto the table's seat and plopped beside him, and he suddenly felt like he was fourteen again and trying to figure out how to get Chelsey Diaz to talk to him without sounding like a complete idiot.

Apparently unaware of his sudden awkwardness, Emily took a sip of her soda as she gazed out over the crowd. "I hope you realize how awesome your family is."

He felt his face warm. "I do. I always have."

"But...?"

"I'm just wired differently. That's all."

"I can understand that," she said. "*Boy*, can I understand that." Then she laughed when the dog twisted to nibble at her chin. "Yes, I know, it's been a while since I've seen you." The puppy yipped and she tilted her head toward Colin. "Have you named him yet?"

He jerked. "No. Since I'm not keeping him. Since I *can't* keep him," he said to her pursed lips. "Can't exactly haul a dog around the world with me. And having to board him all the time...no. You could take him, though."

"Actually...that might be possible now. As soon as I find my own place, that is."

Colin frowned at her. "What?"

She smiled at him, clearly delighted. "The permanent job came through. I'll be working at the gallery during the summer before that, but..." The grin got bigger. "You're looking at Whispering Pines's newest kindergarten teacher."

"Oh. Wow. That's great."

"Thanks. Cannot tell you what a relief that is, since returning to DC would feel like going backward, frankly. And anyway, after what I said to Dad, not to mention my mother..." She pulled a face. "I'm just burning bridges right and left here."

"You don't sound too torn up about that."

"Probably because I'm trying not to think about it too hard. Frankly I pretty much suck at this cutting-the-cord stuff."

He took a sip of his beer. "Got news for you—everyone does."

"Still. I probably could've finessed things with both of them a little better, maybe. However. What's done is done. No place to go from here but up, I suppose." She toyed with the puppy's ears for a moment, then chuckled. "What do you think of *Spud*?"

"Excuse me?"

"As a name." She lifted the dog to face her, chuckling at his rapid-fire darting tongue. "Because you look like a little potato."

Despite the roiling in his head, Colin pushed out a laugh. "You do realize he's not gonna stay that size, right?"

"Which will make the name even funnier. But only if you approve."

"Me?"

"Sure. Since he's your dog, too."

"*Spud's* fine," he said, not looking at her. Then she released a huge sigh. "What was that for?"

"Now that I'm going to be a doggy mama again, it's made me think even more about my own parents. Our strange relationship. I mean, I know they want the best for me. But that's not necessarily what *is* best for me, if you know what I mean."

"I do, actually. Although I'm not sure which is scarier— how your brain works, or that I *get* how your brain works."

Emily laughed, then took a sip of her soda. "Love is such a strange thing, isn't it? I thought I loved my parents, because that's what you do, isn't it? And it's not as if they were ever actually mean to me or beat me or anything. So why wouldn't I love them? Like I thought I loved Michael."

"So you're really over him?"

Cuddling the dog, she shrugged, a gesture that came across a lot sadder than she probably thought it did. "I've accepted that what I thought we had wasn't real. Is that the same as being over him? I'm not entirely sure."

And he knew all about that, didn't he? How rarely logic and emotions saw eye to eye? Suddenly fury roared through Colin, that this sweet, crazy-good person hadn't been loved the way she deserved to be loved. And he wished...

No. You don't.

Because let's listen to the logical side, shall we? That the woman who'd just admitted she wasn't entirely sure she was over her ex didn't need...complications.

As in, him.

"For what it's worth?" he said softly. "I have complete faith in you, that you'll figure it all out."

She turned to him, and what he saw in those pretty blue eyes, that smile, knotted him up inside so badly he could barely breathe. "Oh, yeah?"

"Yeah."

Nodding, she turned away, nuzzling the pup again. "I'd love to see the book. If you're good with that, I mean."

And wasn't it strange that, despite the fact that a whole bunch of people would see it eventually, the thought of *her* seeing it gave him the willies? Because none of those people—editors and marketing people and the like—knew him. None of those people, he didn't think, would read between the lines like he strongly suspected Emily would.

Would see through the thin veneer that separated his public persona from his soul. What passed for his soul, anyway.

"Not sure how much there is to see. That makes sense, anyway. It's mostly a bunch of essays to go with the pics on my computer. The production team will make it all pretty."

"So that's a no?" she said, humor shimmering through her words.

There. She'd offered him the perfect out. All he had to do was accept it—

"It's a... Don't expect a finished product."

"I won't." She awkwardly lowered the pup to the ground, where he raised his nose to the fragrant breeze... and promptly piddled. Chuckling, Emily lifted her gaze, tilting her can toward Zach and Mallory. "Those two are so cute together it almost hurts to watch."

"Truth," he said, and she laughed again, then sobered.

"This was supposed to be my wedding day, too."

His head snapped around to her, although she wasn't looking at him. "Oh, hell..."

"No, it's okay, I'm fine. Especially when I remind myself how horrible it would've been to have found out the truth after we'd gotten married. Maybe after we'd had a kid or two. So no regrets here," she said, lifting the can in a toast to no one in particular. "Believe me."

"And why am I tempted to sniff that can to see what's really in it?"

Emily snorted another little laugh. But again, he heard the sadness. Regret? Perhaps not. Not for him to say, at least. But something he recognized all too well. Then she set the can on the table before leaning back to rest her palms behind her, a move that stretched the lightweight material across her breasts, her thighs, a belly that was all the more enticing for not being completely flat, and he thought at this rate his libido was going to have a stroke. In spite—or maybe because—of the way her expression mellowed.

"You're really at peace here, aren't you?" he asked.

The kindness, the genuineness in her expression when her eyes met his made him ache. More. "I really am. Or at least I'm pretty sure here is where I'll find it." She arched her neck to look up at the sky, and every drop of spit in his mouth evaporated. Especially when a strand of hair toyed with her throat. "But let me guess..." Sitting up again, she linked her hands around her knees. "You're absolutely itching to get away again."

Perhaps *itch* wasn't the best word to bring up right now, when at the moment it applied equally to two entirely conflicting needs. Once more he angled away from that trenchant gaze. "Something like that."

But not for the reasons she thought. Although at least he could be grateful that nobody knew what he'd been considering. Now, however, with Emily staying...

"It must be nice, to be able to go with the flow like that," she said. A gentle laugh washed over him. "I actually envy your sense of adventure."

"Don't," he said, startling himself. "It's not always that great."

He could feel her gaze on the side of his face before she reached for her drink again and took a long swallow. "You mean, because of what you've seen?"

He paused. "Yes."

She jiggled the soda, making the fizzing carbonation ping against the inside of the can. "Thank you."

His brows crashed together as he faced her again. "For what?"

"For trusting me enough to admit that." The space between her own brows creased before her gaze caressed his, a blush sweeping across her cheeks. "I'm just putting this out there, okay? Since I know how hard it can be to talk to the people who know you *too* well. Or think they do, anyway. Because that opens the door to all this advice. Or judgment. Whatever. However…"

Her fingers on his wrist were smooth. Warm. "I also know how crappy it is keeping stuff inside. How it sits there, festering, becoming worse and worse the more you think about it. So if you need someone to talk to…"

"I don't."

She removed her hand, and Colin had to force himself not to grab it back. "Fine. But if you change your mind, I can promise you, no advice. And certainly no judgment."

A frown biting into his forehead, Colin let his gaze swing back to her profile. "Why?"

"Because…because in the past few weeks you've let me *be* me more than anyone else ever has. Except Dee, maybe. But that's different. You didn't have to. Seems only fair to return the favor. And the best part?" Smiling, she met his eyes again, and he could have sworn he saw something in them that had nothing to do with what she was actually saying. Although that could have been wishful thinking on his part. "Once we go back to our lives, we'll probably never see each other again. So there's that. But even, um, a momentary connection is better than nothing."

That last sentence had been spoken so softly, so gently, Colin almost wondered if he'd imagined it. He looked back out over the yard, at the kids running around, the smoke curling up from the giant grill, the normalcy blanketing a moment that he had a strong suspicion had just zoomed so far past normal it wasn't even recognizable anymore.

Except it was. If you knew what you were looking for.

"Are we still talking about…talking?"

Another laugh slapped his libido clear into the next week. Then Emily slid off the table, the move shifting her hem so he got a good long glimpse of gorgeous long leg before she faced him again.

"This is me going with the flow." Her breasts rose with her deep breath. "Seizing a moment."

"Being reckless."

"That, too. But the great thing about knowing what the possibilities are—or aren't—from the get-go, is that there are no expectations. So you can relax and enjoy that moment."

By this point Colin's blood was pumping so hard he could barely hear her. Then he frowned. "Were you... Did you have this in mind when you came out here?"

Her mouth twitched. "Maybe."

He punched out a breath. "Emily... I can't take advantage of you."

"Not asking you to. But, hey, if you don't want to—"

"*Want* has nothing to do with it."

She glanced away, then back at him. "Actually, it has everything to do with it. With...whatever's in your eyes. The stuff you're not telling me. That I'm not asking you to." A half smile curved her mouth. "I can keep your secrets, Colin," she said, her gaze hooked in his. "But I'm good with you keeping them, too."

Then she walked away, that stupid, shapeless dress leaving everything to his imagination.

Which had taken flight like nobody's business.

Chapter Nine

Emily could feel Colin's gaze on her back, five times hotter than the setting sun slicing across the vast yard. And almost hotter than the blush searing her cheeks at what'd just happened.

That she'd come on to a man. With reasonable grace, even.

Although knowing there was no future for them actually made it easier to consider the one thing she'd never before considered in her life—sex simply for fun. For *now*. Because for so many months the implication had been that it'd be some sort of prize for after the wedding, which she'd gone along with because she'd thought the *real* prize was worth the wait.

How wrong she'd been. How very, very wrong.

Oddly—or maybe not—Colin stayed out of her way for the rest of the evening. Although whether because he didn't want his family playing any guessing games, or because he'd found her suggestion utterly abhorrent, she had no idea. Since he hadn't exactly leaped at the opportunity, had he? Still. Nothing ventured, nothing gained and all that. She was hardly going to get her panties in a wad over something that had been a huge gamble to begin with.

Which did not mean her heart didn't whomp up against her ribs like a boss when she got a text from him the next evening, as she sat outside on the Vista's veranda, cocooned against the evening chill in some old shawl of Dee's.

Okay.

Man of few words, that one. Although she might feel a teensy bit more confident with a little expansion. Especially since it had been more than twenty-four hours since she'd tossed down the gauntlet.

Okay, what?

To your suggestion.

Her heart thudded again. She took a deep, deep breath in some lame attempt to steady it, then texted.

You sure?

Roughly a million years later, her phone dinged.

Are you?

And, a second after that:

And yes, I'm giving you an out.

Holy hell. Never, ever in her life had she done anything

like this. Or wanted to. Then again, she'd never been in a situation like this before, had she?

I'll be over in a minute, she texted, then slipped her phone into her jeans pocket before he could respond.

She found Dee and Josh in the great room, cuddled together on one of the couches watching TV. Both kids had zonked out some time ago, their parents' relief obvious on their faces.

"Colin just texted. He says the pup's acting weird. He wants me to come take a look."

Amazing, how easily the lie slid right off her tongue.

Josh glanced up, the light from the screen flickering across his face. "Maybe I should come, too," he said, starting to rise. "Make sure it's nothing serious—"

"And Em can let you know if it is," Dee said, clamping one hand around her husband's forearm and giving Emily a knowing look. Because she was no good whatsoever at this clandestine stuff.

Although Josh, bless his heart, was clearly clueless. "Okay. But I'm here if you need me."

"Thanks." Then she boot-scooted out of there before anyone could see her burning face.

Wrapped more tightly in the shawl, she clomped across the wooden porch, the sound then muffled in the dirt as she made her way past the paddock to the foreman's cabin. The clear, starry night was silent and still, save for the thrum of crickets' chirping, the distant howl of a coyote. The cabin's front door swung open before she reached Colin's porch, a spear of light guiding her way. And with that, the full ramification of what she was doing—or about to do, anyway—slammed into her.

But she had no idea what it might mean to Colin, she thought as his broad-shouldered silhouette filled the doorway, fragmenting the light. Maybe nothing, really—oh, hell, her heart was about to pound right out of her chest, since men were much more adept at these things than women. Weren't they?

Spudsy scampered out onto the porch from behind Colin's feet, wriggling up a storm when he saw her, and Emily's heart stopped its whomping long enough to squeeze at the sight of the bundle of furry joy she'd come to love.

At least she'd be able to keep the dog, she thought as she scooped up the little dog to bury her face in his ruff, trying to ignore Colin's piercing gaze.

Oh, hell. That whole sex-as-fun thing? Who was she kidding? That wasn't her. Never had been. What on earth had made her think a single event would change *her*?

Although this one just might.

"I made a fire," Colin said quietly. Carefully. As though afraid she might spook. Never mind this had been her idea.

"That's nice."

Ergh.

Something like a smile ghosted around his mouth. "We can always just talk. No expectations. Isn't that what you said?" He shoved his hands in his pockets. "You're safe, honey. With me." His lips curved. "*From* me."

Still cuddling the puppy, she came up onto the porch. Closer. Too close. But not so close that she couldn't, if she were so inclined, still grab common sense by the hand and run like hell.

"And from myself?"

"That, I can't help you with."

Another step closer. Then another, each one a little farther away from common sense, whimpering in the dust behind her. "Kiss me," she whispered.

There was so much ambivalence in his smile she almost withdrew her request.

Almost.

* * *

Her mouth was soft and sweet and giving under his, as Colin threaded his fingers through all that shiny, slippery hair to still her trembling. Or maybe to still his—right now he couldn't tell. Her lips parted, trusting; he cautiously accepted her invitation, not wanting to lose that trust. He still wasn't sure of her motivation, but he damn well knew she was still hurting. If he could, even in some small way, ease that ache, even if only a little...

Even if for only a little while...

The dog yipped between them, making them laugh, breaking the tension.

"That was nice," he said, and she smiled.

"Very," she said, that twinkle he'd come to like so much reappearing in her eyes, almost but not quite banishing her obvious uncertainty.

He brushed a kiss across her temple, her sigh making his shudder. "What do you want? Really?"

She angled her head to meet his gaze, her pale neck tempting. "You," she said. "This. Now."

"You sure?"

"Yes."

But he caught the momentary hesitation before her response.

Colin slid a hand to her waist, led her through the open door. Even though he wasn't a total slob—he couldn't work in a pigsty—he'd made even more of an effort to straighten up. Because this mattered. *She* mattered.

Emily lowered the puppy to the floor; he immediately toddled into his crate, curled up like a little bean and passed out.

Good dog.

Hugging herself, Emily released a strained laugh. "I

told Dee and Josh you said the dog was acting funny, that I should come check on him."

"And did they buy that?"

"Your brother, maybe. Dee? Not so much."

"Yeah, I'm thinking you probably suck at poker," he said, and another shaky chuckle pushed from her throat. "Look, Emily—"

Then her hands were on his chest, those guileless eyes hooked in his. "And the longer we chitchat, the more nervous I'm going to get. So can we get on with it, already?"

"And aren't you the sweet-talker?"

"I'm sorry—"

"No." He took her hands, folding them both over his pounding heart. "But I'm not entirely sure why you want to do this."

"Do I need a reason?"

"If any other woman had asked me that, I'd say no. Only you're not any other woman. Yes, I know what you said, about this being for the moment and all. And while *I'm* good with that, I'm not entirely sure you are. Not as much as you might think—"

"Colin—"

"No, let me finish, so there's no room for misinterpretation, on either side. I won't hurt you, not if I can help it. But I have no control over what might happen inside your head."

Or mine, he thought, immediately adding, *Oh, hell, no.*

A sly, if none too steady, grin spread across her face. "Because you're just that irresistible, you mean?"

Again, the tension eased. "It has been said," he said, and she laughed, full out. And linked her hands around the back of his neck, bringing their pelvises together, and things stirred, eager as hell…and he picked her up and carried her to the bedroom, leaving regrets scattered behind him like confetti after a parade. Then she murmured, "Und-dress me. Please," and his heart knocked against his ribs at the slight stumble, like he might decline for some reason.

Because clearly someone else had.

"So is this revenge sex?"

Her gaze darkened. "No. Never."

He believed her. "Then...with pleasure," he whispered back, taking his time, bending to remove her boots before letting his fingers deliberately tease silk-slick skin as he removed her sweater, both of them chuckling when her hair went all staticky. Her bra was plainer than he'd expected, but sheer, her nipples trapped beneath the shimmery nude fabric. With a single flick of the front clasp he could free them, if he wanted. Give them air, give him one of many ways to make her moan. Make both of them very, very happy.

But not yet.

Torture is what this was, what he was doing to himself, to her, going so slowly. Holding back. And yet with each touch, each glance, each hitch of her breath as he unzipped her jeans, tugging them down to carefully kiss first one hip bone, then the other, he ached more, *wanted* more.

But more than anything he wanted to give her everything she'd given up for some schmuck who'd never deserved her.

Not that he did, either. But at least he could give her this.

"Step out," he murmured, guiding her out of the jeans and tossing them aside before pressing his lips to the top of her panties, the same sheer fabric as her bra. Then lower, making her gasp.

And laugh. With delight, he thought. Anticipation. Good.

He stood to claim her mouth again, the kiss so deep and tender and full of promise he nearly wept, and he picked

her up again, her legs tightly wrapped around his waist—
speaking of promise—and carried her to the bed before
lowering her onto the mattress. Then he finally unclasped
the bra, sighing at her beauty, pale rose against flawless
ivory, only to feel his throat close up when he caught her
gaze in his, that mixture of hesitation and bravado that
would be his undoing.

"Now you," she whispered.

He toed off his sneakers, shrugged out of his shirt, his
jeans—

"Commando?" she said, that smile playing around her
lips. "I'm impressed." Her gaze lowered. "Very impressed."

"Careful. You'll give me a swelled…" He grinned.
"Head."

"Oh, jeez," she said, rolling her eyes, then got to her
knees on the mattress to link her hands behind his neck
again, and the feel of all that softness, skin to skin…that
mouth—oh, merciful heavens, that *mouth*, on his neck,
his chest…

"A year, you said?"

Chuckling, she raised herself up again, skimming her
fingers through his hair. "Longer, now. But some things,
you don't forget. Although…" Her eyes melted into his,
and he was a goner. "You inspire me."

He gripped her waist. Tugged her closer. She was still
wearing her panties, an oversight he needed to remedy
ASAP. "To do what?" he teased.

Something more serious flickered in her eyes. "Give
more," she whispered, running the tip of her tongue along
his jaw. "Do more." She pulled back again, her lips barely
curved. "*Be* more."

"And if you were any *more*," Colin said, lowering her
to the bed again, "my head might explode."

Her eyes glittered again. "I thought that was the idea."

Chuckling, he positioned her beneath him to finally pay some attention to those lovely breasts, as rapidly mounting need trampled regrets underfoot. Even though he knew how resilient those suckers could be. He hooked his fingers around the panties, eased them off. "And maybe I should stop talking now."

"Works for me," she said, and then there was nothing between them except touches and sighs, the occasional gasp…kisses finding their way to secret places, lingering and hot…quiet *yeses* leading to the guttural sounds of pure, perfect pleasure as he held her hands over her head and plunged inside her, her tightness more than making up for the condom's barrier between them.

Colin watched her expression morph from anticipation to wonder, then complete submission to the moment as her cries rang out in the small room, until she wrapped herself tightly around him and pulled him close, closer, taking him inside her in far more ways than one, as *This, I can give you*, whispered through his brain.

Only, when they were done, as he tugged her close to lay his cheek in her hair, feeling his heart pound against hers, he realized what an idiot he'd been, thinking he could give her this and not give her…

Himself.

Except that wasn't possible, was it?

Emily knew, even before the tremors died down, that everything she'd suspected—okay, had already known—about her not being one of those people who could use sex as simply a recreational activity was absolutely true. And not because of the whole swapping-bodily-fluids thing that supposedly bonded a woman to her man, or whatever, because Colin had insisted on using a condom. Even though she'd told him that wasn't necessary.

Which made her wonder how much more bonded she'd be feeling right now if they *hadn't* used one. Scary thought.

Of course, she thought as he tugged her closer, his fingers making slow, sweet circles on her shoulder as they lay snuggled together like a pair of baby rabbits, what she might be *feeling* had nothing to do with what was actually going to happen. That much she'd known going in. No changing the ground rules after the fact. Although—her practical side weighed in—why should she be surprised, really? She'd only recently been jilted/dumped/betrayed/done wrong, for one thing. Add to that the fact that it'd been a while…and add to *that* the fact that Colin was quite possibly the world's most attentive lover and…

Right.

Seriously, this was the confluence of events to beat all confluences. She wasn't in love with the man, she was just…mellow. That's all.

Incredibly, wonderfully, out-of-body-experience mellow.

Except she needed to pee. Bummer.

"Where you going?" Colin asked as she shimmied out from under his arm, grabbing his shirt off the floor before shrugging into it.

"Bathroom."

"Hey."

She turned back, holding the shirt closed over her breasts.

"You okay?"

Her cheeks ached with her forced smile. "You really have to ask?"

Frowning, he stretched his arms to fold his hands behind his head, the sheet barely covering the good bits. What was behind that frown, she didn't want to know.

Didn't need to. So she'd reassure him…as soon as she got back.

When she returned, however, he'd gone into the living room, his jeans back on and zipped but not buttoned as he stood in front of the desk, his laptop opened.

"You said you wanted to see the book," he said, not looking at her, and she felt as though a storm had come up suddenly, sucking all the air out of the space.

"Um…sure."

He turned then, his smile sad. But his eyes… Oh, dear God. *Tortured* was the only word for what she saw in them. He gestured toward the chair in front of the computer.

"Sit. Although like I said," he said when she did, "it's only a rough draft."

She laughed, although the sound was hollow. "You expect me to read the whole thing tonight?"

"I can send you the file, if you'd like. But this chapter…" He leaned close enough for her to smell herself on him, which naturally awakened the barely quenched ache all over again. "You should probably read this now."

The chapter focused on one particular group of refugees he'd apparently spent some time with, enough to get to know them fairly well. The pictures, especially, kept coming back to one little boy—the kid she'd seen before. Then she read on, about a virus of some kind that swept through the makeshift camp, claiming mostly children—malnourished, exhausted children whose immune systems simply couldn't fight off the microbes' relentless assault.

Tears welled in her eyes, even as her stomach knotted, knowing what was coming. "The boy—"

"An orphan," Colin said from behind her, seated on the sofa. She turned, her soul weeping at his ravaged expression. The pup had awakened and was sitting on Colin's lap, offering whatever comfort he could. Colin heaved out a breath. "Tarik's parents had been murdered by militants. Friends had somehow smuggled him out of the country, even though they had no idea where they might even end up." He paused, toying with the puppy's ears before meeting her gaze again, the corners of his mouth pushed into something like a smile. "For reasons I never fully understood, the kid glommed on to me. He'd follow me around, asking questions about the camera. In makeshift sign language, of course, since we didn't exactly speak each other's language. But…"

"But you fell in love with him."

"Head over heels."

"How old was he?"

"Six." He hauled in a shaky breath. "The UN workers at the camp knew me. One of them called me the day he died."

On a soft moan, Emily went to him, curling up on the sofa to wrap her arm around his waist. To his credit, Colin accepted her meager, and futile, attempt to comfort him, lifting his arm to pull her close, kiss her hair.

"That's the real reason you came home, isn't it?" she said after a long moment. "The book…that was simply an excuse."

"A convenient excuse, but…yeah."

The weird thing was, she understood why he'd chosen to seek sanctuary in the very place he'd refused to come back to for so long—because for all Colin's noise about how much he'd felt restricted here, he'd also felt the same peace that now made her want to call Whispering Pines home, too. Maybe he wouldn't—or couldn't—admit that, but when you need to heal you don't run someplace you *don't* like. In a way, she realized, he'd become like one of the kids he—and his horse, Jack—had helped all those years ago.

But there was more, wasn't there?

"And what happened…that's why you don't want children? Now, I mean."

A long moment of silence preceded, "I felt like I broke a promise to him. And I know that's illogical, especially since I didn't actually make a promise, not in so many words. I couldn't adopt him myself…how on earth would I take care of a kid on my own? Still, the way he'd wrapped himself around my heart, I would've done whatever I could to…"

"Colin," Emily said gently, twisting to rest a hand on his cheek, her insides more twisted up than his expression. "You can't blame yourself for something that was totally out of your control—"

"Except I *knew* not to let it get personal, that the moment I lost my objectivity, I was screwed. Even if I had no idea how much." Sensing that wasn't all, Emily kept quiet, waiting for him to gather his thoughts. His words. "It was hard for me to even admit to myself, let alone anyone else, how much his death shattered me. With all the crap I've seen, I'm not exactly a wuss. But that…it threw me. Bad."

Emily nuzzled her cheek against his chest, inhaling his scent. His warmth. Wishing she could somehow absorb some of his anguish. "And your breakup…?"

Her face lifted with his breath. "Happened a few months before. I hadn't realized how hard I'd fallen for her, either. That, though, I could get over. And had, mostly. But watching so many people go through hell… I thought I'd become inured to it. I was wrong."

"And yet…" She sat up to meet his eyes. "You want to go back."

A sad smile preceded, "I have to. To honor Tarik, if nothing else."

Emily thought for a moment, frowning. "Even though

you don't want to open yourself up to that kind of pain again. I don't mean just witness it. I mean let yourself experience it."

What felt like an eternity passed before he said, "I don't think I can. Not if I want to keep doing my job."

"Which you'd die if you couldn't do."

In answer, he tugged her close again. *Yes. That.*

Even so, Emily strongly suspected—especially in the light of what had just happened between them—that *detachment* wasn't even remotely part of this man's skill set, no matter how much he might wish it to be. If it were, he wouldn't be able to do what he loved.

"And all of that was my long-winded way of saying—"

"You can't be the person I need."

Another sigh preceded, "And you have no idea how much I wish I could be. How much I wish…"

For a brief moment, she saw tears gather in his eyes before he pulled her close again, the gesture again saying what he couldn't. That what he wanted, whether he could admit it or not, was in direct conflict with what he needed to do, even after everything he'd seen. And he had no earthly idea how to reconcile the two.

And neither did, *could*, she—a thought that shredded her inside. Because they'd crossed a boundary that should've never been crossed.

That *she* should've never crossed.

"It's okay," Emily said, fighting to keep her voice steady. "I already knew that coming in, remember? Our goals, our plans, our *needs* don't mesh. This was…" She cleared her throat. "This was never meant to be anything more than what it was."

"I'm sorry—"

"For *what*, for heaven's sake?" Twisting around to straddle his lap, she cupped his jaw in her hands. "For making me feel more *cared* about tonight than anyone else ever has?"

That got another gut-shredding smile. "That was the idea."

"And a damn fine one it was, too. So thank you," Emily whispered, brushing her lips across his, her skin sweetly sighing when his hands skimmed her bare waist underneath his shirt. She shoved her hair back over her shoulder and smiled into his eyes. "Because if nothing else, you have seriously raised my standards—"

From several feet away, she heard her phone ding.

"You should probably see to that," Colin said. Even though his thumbs were stroking the undersides of her breasts.

"Why?"

"Because if it's your cousin and you don't answer, she's likely to jump to conclusions."

"And I think that falls under the category of 'too late, buster.'" But she crawled off the man's lap—reluctantly—and took her grumbling hormones over to the other side of the room and picked up her phone, frowning at the text from her cousin.

You should probably get back.

Accompanied by a pic of her mother standing in the ranch's great room.

And looking very, very pissed.

Chapter Ten

"What is it?" Colin said behind her, his murmured words jarring her enough out of her shock to think, *Oh, hell.*

"My mother just showed up," she said, heading back to the bedroom to yank on her own clothes, tossing Colin's shirt on top of the rumpled bedclothes. She caught a glance of herself in the mirror over his dresser and grimaced. Between the rat's-nest hair and the beard burn...

Yeah. *Screwed* was definitely the word of the moment. See, this is why she'd always been the good girl, because she could never get away with a damn thing—

Colin came up behind her to quickly squeeze her shoulders before grabbing the shirt off the bed and punching his arms into the sleeves. "I'm coming with you."

Her fingers tangled in the mop, Emily wheeled around. "Oh, no, you're not—"

"Yes, I am," he said calmly, sitting on the bed to tie his shoelaces. "Because I doubt your mother is either blind or stupid. And the minute you walk through the door at this time of night, looking like that, she's gonna know." He frowned. "You really think I'd let you deal with the fallout by yourself? And before you pull your hair out of your scalp, there's a comb in the bathroom. If you don't mind my cooties."

"I think our cooties are definitely BFFs by now," Emily muttered, then hurried into the tiny en suite and grabbed the comb off the sink. And if she artfully arranged the waves, maybe the red patches wouldn't be so noticeable? No?

Then she glowered at her reflection. *Wait a goshdarn minute...*

Colin was tucking in his shirt when she roared back out of the bathroom, the man's expression remarkably calm for someone who'd been as good as caught with her in a very compromising position. And thank God for that, since *calm* was one thing Emily definitely was not right now.

"What the hell is she doing here anyway?"

"I assume that's a rhetorical question? Although that fury you're feeling right now?" He buckled his belt, then snagged her shawl off the chair and tossed it to her. "Hold on to that. 'Cause something tells me you're gonna need it."

That stopped her. And forced a tight little laugh from her throat. "And it's a lot easier to be angry with someone from two thousand miles away than when they're right in front of you, isn't it?"

"Yep," he said, then reached for her hand. "I have no doubt whatsoever you've got this, baby. But I've also got your back."

She turned to him, fighting the burning sensation in her eyes. "And I repeat, you don't have to do this. Play the white knight or whatever. Especially since...this isn't—wasn't—real."

Something like anger shunted across his features. "You don't think what happened here tonight was *real*?"

For a moment, she was confused. "After everything we just said—"

His grip on her shoulders almost hurt. Although not nearly as much as the regret in those pale green eyes. "This is about *now*, Emily. This moment." She saw the muscles in his throat work. "True, maybe I can't be what you need for the long haul, but sure as hell I'm not pretending like tonight never happened. That it wasn't important. Because believe me, honey...it was. More than you have any idea."

Except, in a blinding, breath-stealing flash...she did. Even, somehow, over all the other crap crashing around underneath her skull.

The turkey was every bit as much in love with her as she was with him.

And compared with the frustrating futility of *that* little situation, dealing with her crazy mother was child's play.

"Should we bring Spud?"

"Why not?" Colin said, whistling for the pup. And as they walked in silence to the main house, the pup tumbling over his big feet, the twinkling stars in the blue-black sky seemed to chuckle at them.

With good reason.

"A little warning would've been nice, Mother," Emily said a few minutes later, after her mother had clearly put two and two together and arrived at *suitably appalled*.

"Clearly," she said, seated across from Emily in the great room, the light from the wrought iron chandelier overhead gleaming in her artfully highlighted auburn hair. The others had retreated to the kitchen, although Colin had refused to leave until Emily promised to let him know if she needed him. Even though she knew that *he* knew she needed to handle this on her own. Because "having your back" came in many different flavors.

"And why are you here, anyway?"

"We'll get to that in a minute." Her mother blew out a breath between lips rimmed with what was left of her signature bright red lipstick. And for a moment Emily felt a twinge of sympathy, that the woman had endured a long travel day, with layovers and the drive here from the airport stretching the trip to nearly twelve hours. Still, no one had asked her to make the trek out here. Least of all Emily. "But for God's sake, Emily—I can't believe you hooked up with someone this soon after your own wedding day."

She supposed, from her mother's point of view, that's exactly what she'd done. And what the hell, she might as well own it. "Except, in case you missed it, I did not, in fact, get married."

Her mother's expression went from *frosty* to *arctic*. "And whose fault was that?"

"You know, I believe we'll have to cede that one to Michael."

"Oh, for heaven's sake, Emily…that's what men *do*. And it's not as if you were married yet."

"And thank God for that. Except, really? That's what men *do*? Or only men you happen to be married to?"

Her mother's face went as red as the lipstick she'd probably chewed off by Dallas. "Your father's always been a good provider. And loyal, in his own way. So I learned to look the other way."

"Oh, jeez, Mother—"

"Your father's and my relationship is none of your business."

"And neither is mine with…well, whoever, actually. Because it's *my* life? Where I get to make my choices?"

That got a hard stare, one that even a few months ago would have made Emily's stomach go wobbly. Now? Nope.

"So, what? This—" her mother waved at the beard burn "—was about, what? Getting even?"

"Actually, it was about being with someone who actually cares about my feelings."

Her mother scoffed. "Oh, please, Emily…you can't be that naive."

"You mean, the way you and Dad raised me?"

"Don't be ridiculous. We didn't—"

"Careful, Mother. Considering a second ago you took me to task for walking away from someone who cheated on me because… What was that you said? Oh, right… 'That's what men do.' So, two things." She crossed her arms. "One, no, they don't. At least not all of them. And two, that naïveté thing? Done."

"I hardly think a fling with a cowboy is a way to prove your maturity. Do you?"

Somehow, Emily steadied her breathing. Somehow, she didn't give in to the impulse to storm out of the room and leave her mother to stew in her own juices. Because that would be playing right into her hand, wouldn't it? Giving her all the ammunition she needed to verify her accusation, her assumption, that Emily was still a child who couldn't be trusted to make her own decisions.

That she was a stupid little girl who needed guidance. Direction.

By the same token, neither was she about to let herself get sucked into an argument, which would give her mother another kind of satisfaction. Funny, how she could almost feel Colin's go-get-'em-tiger from down the hall. The sort of support she'd never felt, not once, the entire time she and Michael had been together.

"Believe it or not," she said quietly, "I wasn't trying to

prove anything. To anybody. All I was doing was living my life, on my terms. Not anyone else's—"

"You can't stay, Emily. And I'm not leaving until you come to your senses."

Her laugh clearly startled her mother. "You seriously came out here to bring me home?"

"Since talking to you over the phone wasn't working… yes."

"And what on earth made you think you'd get a different result in person? Mother… I have a *job*, a commitment I fully intend to honor. I'm not about to leave these people in a lurch simply because you have issues with it. Issues which for the life of me I don't understand—"

"Then let me make it simple for you. You don't belong here. This life…it isn't *your* life. Oh, I know, it might seem like some sort of big adventure right now, but you'll tire of it soon enough, believe me." Her mother tried to soften her voice. It didn't entirely work. "Look, I understand, the whole thing with the wedding getting called off…that's enough to shake anybody up. To make you do… Well, to make you not think straight. Do things you wouldn't do if you were. But if you believe being out here is going to somehow magically fix everything…" Her voice hardened again. But not before Emily caught an unmistakable flash of fear that made her frown. "Don't be a fool, Emily—"

"And I'd stop right there if I were you," Colin quietly said from the doorway. Emily's mother whipped around.

"This is a private conversation, if you don't mind."

"Which was edging a mite too close to abusive for my taste."

Her mother's jaw dropped. "*Abusive?* Are you serious?"

"Colin, it's okay—"

"Not sure what else you'd call it—"

"Both of you! Cut it out!" Emily struggled to her feet,

feeling as though her brain had been stuffed in a blender. "Jeebus. Colin…" She crossed to him to fit her hand in his. Because it wasn't as if this couldn't get any worse, so what the hell? "I appreciate your coming to my defense, but seriously—I don't need it." She turned. "Although, actually, Mother—he's right. All my life you've tried to manipulate me into being who you want me to be, *what* you want me to me, as a reflection of you. It stops now."

"Why, you little ingrate—"

Still hanging on to Colin's hand—Colin's warm, strong hand—Emily held up her free one. "I'm not ungrateful for the things I should be grateful for. Really. I know I had a charmed childhood, that you and Dad gave me everything I ever wanted. But that doesn't mean…" She took a deep breath. "That doesn't mean you own me. Or that I owe you anything *besides* my gratitude…"

But her mother clearly wasn't listening, her gaze instead zeroing in on Colin's hand linked with hers. When she lifted her eyes, Emily saw the fear again, more intensified. "So are you two actually together?"

"No," they said at the same time, and confusion *almost* cramped her mother's Botoxed forehead. Must be time for a tune-up. Emily slid her hand out of Colin's.

"But what we are, or aren't, is frankly none of your business. I tried it your way, Mother," she said before the woman could interrupt. "And it was an unmitigated disaster."

Her mother's gaze zeroed in on Colin before returning to Emily. "And this won't be?" she said quietly, then brushed past Emily on her way out of the room.

After Deanna's filling Colin in on a few things over the past fifteen minutes, neither Margaret Weber's dismissal nor her lobbing the last word as she swept from the room surprised him.

Neither had Emily's standing up to her mother. For herself. Because from that first conversation all those weeks ago he'd glimpsed an inner strength he doubted she'd even been aware of at that point.

A *woman's* strength. That indefatigable resilience that held families together, protected children…stood up to tyranny with no regard for personal safety.

But what had surprised him—as in, rattled him to the core—was his reaction to her courage. Hell, her outright defiance of her mother's domineering attitude. Emily Weber was one tough cookie.

A tough cookie Colin was falling in love with so hard it almost hurt to breathe. And what exactly was he supposed to do with that, for God's sake?

"You were supposed to stay away," Emily said, standing in front of the open French door with her back to him, her arms folded across her ribs. A stiff breeze whisked across the large room, stirring the drapes, rattling papers on the coffee table.

"I couldn't."

"I told you, I didn't need rescuing."

"That wasn't why I couldn't stay away."

Her forehead knotted, she turned. Then, shaking her head, she released a sad little laugh. "Did you feel like this, when you stood up to your father?"

Colin frowned as he rammed his fingers into his back pockets. "Not sure what you mean by 'like this'—"

"Loyalty knocking heads with needing to find yourself. *Be* yourself." Tears glistened in her eyes. "Did it… did it tear you up inside?"

For the first time, he saw what her rebellion was costing her. A realization that only made it even clearer that she didn't need any *more* obstacles tossed in her path to self-discovery.

Never mind that for a moment there, when they were still at the cabin, he'd been tempted to backpedal, to take another stab at something he knew from experience would never work. Because it hadn't before. Because *feelings*, no matter how strong, never trumped logic. Practicality.

Inevitability.

"Some, sure." Then he blew out his own laugh. "Who am I kidding? Of course it did. I love my folks, I think the world of them, and I knew Dad didn't understand what I was doing. What I had to do. But—"

Too late, he caught himself.

"But the family dynamic isn't exactly the same," Emily said. "I know." Heaving a huge sigh, she walked back over to the sofa and dropped onto the edge, her arms tightly crossed over her stomach. "My mother isn't an easy person to love. But I do love her. And she's got her good points. Like taking in Dee after Aunt Kathryn died. Maybe her reasons weren't entirely altruistic, but we were raised like sisters. If anything, Mother might've overcompensated a bit with Dee to—in her mind—make up for what had happened. But…" She blew out another breath. "She never got over her only sister moving so far away, embracing a life she couldn't understand. So I know it's killing her to think I might do the same thing."

Again, Deanna had filled him in a little bit ago, about her aunt's issues with Whispering Pines. Even though Colin's reasons for not wanting to stay were entirely different from Margaret Weber's old fears about her sister, he still had to sympathize with her, at least to some extent.

"This really feels like home?"

Emily's gaze met his. "It really does. Yes, I love your family, and the landscape—the obvious things. But it goes beyond that. It simply…feels right. Feels like me." A small smile touched her still-swollen lips. "It always did, even when I was a kid."

Then she got to her feet and slowly walked over to him to wrap her arms around his waist, and he felt his heart crack. "I know, to you, this probably seems like I'm settling. That I've chosen something small and quiet and safe. Except..." She sighed. "When I look into those children's eyes in the classroom, or when I see the love all these people have for each other, how they show it, every minute of every day... to me, that feels pretty darn big."

Colin tugged her close, his own eyes burning as he pressed his cheek against her hair. "Reminds me of what my dad said to me," he whispered, "when I told him I was leaving. But I can't—"

"I know," she murmured into his chest, then leaned back to look up at him, tears brimming on her lower lashes. "And I totally understand. Believe me. Different purposes, different paths..." She shrugged. "That's how it goes sometimes. Nobody's fault." Then she snuggled close again. "Doesn't mean my heart's not breaking right now."

"I know what you mean," he pushed out, holding on to her as tightly as he dared before saying, praying his voice held, "I'll take the pup back for tonight, but Josh said I could leave him here tomorrow morning."

Then, with another kiss to her soft, soft hair, he let her go.

Holding on to her shaking self as though she'd fly into a million pieces if she didn't, Emily watched Colin walk away, wondering if she'd even ever see him again. A thought she let play through a dozen times, simply to torture herself. Because she didn't need to hear the words to know he'd be gone by tomorrow, if not before. Why else would he be bringing Spud here in the morning? After all, there was no reason for him to stick around, now that the book was done. And even though she'd laid bare her soul just now—because he deserved to know the truth about how she felt—not only was that not a reason for him to stay, if anything she'd given him that final little push to leave sooner rather than later. Would she ever willingly hurt him? Of course not. But he didn't know that, did he?

How it was even possible that she'd fallen in love, and so hard, in such a short time she had no idea. Especially after what she'd just been through. But she had. And now, standing in the vast room by herself, she blew out a dry laugh, that her mother had been right. Not that whatever had happened between her and Colin even remotely compared with the ignominious end to a three-year relationship with someone she'd expected to spend the rest of her life with. This one at least had come with a built-in end date, one they'd both been fully aware of from the beginning. So humiliation wasn't even an issue.

Pain, however…

Emily sat back on the sofa, her legs tucked up underneath her, realizing the only person she wanted to talk to about her feelings was the only person she couldn't. That if nothing else, she'd found a friend in Colin, a *good* friend, someone she knew she could trust with her life.

And had, whether she wanted to admit that or not.

"Oh, sweetie…"

She hadn't heard Dee come in. Or realized she was crying until a box of tissues plopped on the sofa beside her a moment before her cousin followed suit—the only other true friend she'd ever had. The only other person she knew she could trust with her life, her sorrows, her secrets.

Dee wrapped Emily up in her arms and tugged her close, much the same way Emily had for her only a few months before when her cousin's world had shattered, as well.

"You slept with him, didn't you?"

There wasn't the slightest trace of judgment in her cousin's gently spoken words. And not only because considering Dee's history she had no room to talk, but because that had never been part of their relationship, anyway. Not with each other. Although remembering their conversation that first night, Emily pushed out a puny little laugh.

"Hey," she said, a soggy tissue clutched in her fist. "It was your idea."

"Yeah, well, that was on a par with 'Why *not* eat the whole cheesecake?' Fun to think about, major regrets after you've actually done it."

"Speak for yourself," Emily grumbled, and Dee chuckled. Then Emily pushed herself upright, partly to grab another tissue, partly to get hold of herself. "I did know what I was getting into. Except I never thought…"

"You'd fall for this insanely good, and good-looking, man who's the diametric opposite of the schmuck who screwed you over? No, I bet you never saw that coming." At Emily's pathetic little laugh, Dee said, "So what do you want to do?"

"Besides eat that cheesecake, you mean? What *can* I do? Colin doesn't feel… He doesn't want what I do, Dee. Family, home." Her mouth pulled flat. "A quiet life. And he especially doesn't want any of that here."

"And you're sure about that?"

"I can only go by what the man said."

Except…deep down, she suspected he did want those things. Even if he hadn't figured out how to make the pieces fit.

Or how to handle whatever the fear was that made him believe he didn't.

Letting her head drop back onto the buttery, cushioned leather, Emily blew a breath toward the beamed ceiling.

"It's crazy, how up until a few weeks ago I hadn't fully realized how much I was living someone else's life. Being who other people wanted me to be. Other than my teaching, I mean. Aside from that..." Her head rolled sideways, her gaze meeting her cousin's. "It was almost as if I'd made a bargain of sorts, with my parents—'Let me do this, and I'll give you everything else. Give you myself.' Then, with Michael, I even gave up teaching. In exchange for the family I thought I was going to have. But it was all a crock, wasn't it? An illusion."

A tight smile pushed at her mouth when she felt Dee's hand fold around hers. "So I came out here to figure out who I really was. What I really wanted. Instead I found..." She almost laughed. "The real version of everything I thought I already had. Who I *already* was. So here I am, finally living what feels like a truly genuine life, *my* life, someplace that finally feels like home..."

Emily pushed herself off the couch to close the French doors before they froze to death, only to stand facing outside, still grasping the door handles. "Not gonna lie, right now it's tempting—*so* tempting—to revert to that obedient little girl who'd do whatever it took to make someone like me. Accept me." She faced her cousin again, sitting backward on the sofa, sympathy shining in her eyes. "To suck it up, to *give* up what I've only just found in order to be whoever Colin might need me to be. Even though I know that's not even possible. But giving *him* up...it hurts, Dee. Oh, God, it hurts."

"More than Michael?"

"God, yes," she said on an ugly laugh. "As crazy as that sounds. But for one thing, I know Colin wouldn't let me do that. Any more than I'd expect him to change who he is, or not follow his path, for me. Because..." Her eyes stinging, she shook her head. "Finding the right person doesn't mean losing yourself. Or shouldn't, anyway. Something that's taken me twenty-seven years to figure out. Damned if I'm going to throw all that away now. But honestly—to finally find someone who actually gives a damn about what I think, how *I* feel, what *I* need to be, only to realize..." Emily pressed a hand to her mouth, then dropped it again. "Only to realize we want different things...man, that sucks."

Her own eyes brimming, Dee got up to pull Emily into her arms, the second time that evening someone Emily loved with all her heart had hugged her.

But whoever said hugs were always comforting was talking out of their butt.

"The thing is, dog... I know I'm doing the right thing."

The puppy sat in front of him on the floor, head cocked. Damn, he was gonna miss the little turkey. But—

"Because the sooner I leave, the faster Emily'll get over me and get on with her new life." A life, from the sound of things, she'd chosen for herself for once. "Right?"

The pup yipped, then bounced over to crawl into his lap and start gnawing on his fingers. And of course Colin immediately thought of the dog's doing the same thing to Emily, of her grins and giggles when he did, of how she didn't care one whit about puppy slobber on her face.

And he was here in the living room instead of in the bedroom, packing, because it still smelled of her in there. Felt like her. And, yes, he went ahead and tormented himself with thinking about how a couple hours ago he'd been inside her, feeling her pulse around him, hearing her soft cries in his ears, then that damned laughter when it was over, so fricking pleased with herself.

With him.

About how perfect sex wasn't about crazy-ass contortions that only left you with pulled muscles, anyway—it was about being with the right person.

No matter how wrong she was. You know, from a logical perspective.

The pup yipped again, then squirmed around to flip upside down in Colin's lap, showing off his spotted tummy.

"You're right, I'm an idiot—"

At the tentative knock on his door, his stomach lurched. Not his brother's knock, that was for sure, since Josh was more of a pounder than a rapper. But if it was Emily...

He'd deal. Somehow.

Shoving himself to his feet, he crossed the room, taking care not to step on the dancing dog who clearly thought he was playing. He hauled in a breath, plastered on a neutral expression and opened the door.

"We need to talk," Emily's mother said, then pushed her way inside.

Chapter Eleven

Because his psyche hadn't been battered enough. Got it.

"About—?" Colin said, slugging his hands in his pockets and slapping on a neutral expression. He hoped.

"Is there somewhere you can put the dog?" Margaret asked, scowling down at the pup. Who was bowing before her, butt in the air, tail a blur.

"You allergic?"

"No, but…" Eyes nearly the same color as Emily's, but colder, harder, met his. "But he's—"

"A dog. Who'll probably pass out in a minute, not to worry."

Her gaze still fixed on the pup, Emily's mother pushed her chin-length hair behind her ear. And smiled. Not a warm, boundless grin, like her daughter would give. But the corners of her mouth definitely turned up. "A little undisciplined for my taste," she said, more to herself than him, Colin suspected. "But cute. I don't suppose you have any tea?"

"Yes. Which I have no compunction about holding hostage until you tell me why you're here."

That actually got a laugh. "You drive a hard bargain," she said, which was when Colin realized a Southern accent soft-edged her words. The pup attacked the toe of what was probably a very expensive flat shoe. In a single move, the woman bent over to gather him into her arms, where he promptly snuggled in and went to sleep. Huh. "My daughter doesn't know I'm here."

"Didn't figure she did."

"And you're going to make this difficult, aren't you?"

Colin crossed his arms. "Out of deference to not only my parents, but your daughter, I'll try not to be rude. But my loyalty is to Emily. And you still haven't answered my question."

A long, harsh intake of breath preceded, "That girl's already had her heart broken once this year. The thought of it happening again, especially so soon after the first time, breaks mine. In spite of whatever it is you might think about me, and/or my relationship with my daughter."

The woman had been in his space less than five minutes and had already surprised him three times. Not that he was about to let her know that.

"And your point is?"

"Oh, for God's sake, young man—please do not play the fool with me. Emily's obviously in love with you. Only she seems convinced the two of you can't work it out."

A long moment passed before, deciding she'd earned her tea, Colin yanked his gaze from hers and went into the kitchen to pull out assorted boxes of tea bags. Placing them on the counter between the two rooms, he indicated for Emily's mother to make her choice. A moment passed before she pointed to what she apparently deemed the least offensive, then set down the puppy before hiking herself onto a stool on the living room side to watch Colin as he poured water into a mug, set it in the microwave.

"So what I've gathered thus far," he said as the microwave whirred behind him, "is that you're worried I'll break your daughter's heart. Although whether because you're afraid I'll stay or leave I haven't quite worked out yet. Let alone what you'd like me to do to remedy the situation."

"Can you even do that?"

He felt his mouth tuck up on one side. "Assuage your guilt about what happened before, you mean?"

"You sure don't pull any punches, do you?"

"Not if I can help it." The microwave dinged; he pulled out the steaming mug, dunking the bag into it before setting it in front of the woman, along with a sugar bowl. She looked at it like he'd offered her arsenic.

"To tell you the truth, I'm not entirely sure why I'm here. Let alone what I expect, or want, the outcome to be. All I know is there's been far too little truth telling in this family over the last thirty years. And when I overheard Emily talking to her cousin a little while ago... I guess I didn't fully realize how much damage her father and I had done. Not that we meant to—we both love her, I swear— but sometimes when parents are so focused on what *they* think is best for their child, they totally miss what the child really wants. And needs. Especially when..." Staring at her tea, Margaret huffed a sigh. "When the parents have royally screwed up their own lives. Of course the irony is, the more things go wrong, the more you think you can fix them by repeating the same mistakes."

She finally lifted the mug, only to set it down again without tasting the tea. "I want to think Emily's *fascination* with being out here stems from her being unhappy with, well, all sorts of things, I suppose. Things I don't think she even knew she was unhappy with until this craziness with Michael. But now it occurs to me, she was living a lie, wasn't she? A lie her father and I perpetuated, all in the name of appearances. So what I'm saying is…she's vulnerable. A lot more vulnerable than I realized. And I should've done more, to protect her, to keep her from…"

Her mouth clamped shut, Margaret lifted her tea again. Although more to hide behind the mug than to take a drink, Colin suspected.

"To keep her from making the same mistake you believe your sister did."

The woman's eyes shot to his. "What do you know about that?"

"Only what Deanna told me. About how upset you were when Deanna's mother married her father, made her home out here—"

"Away from her real life, yes. It killed her, you know. Or maybe you don't."

He knew enough, although Deanna hadn't been specific. But what it boiled down to was that Deanna's mother had made a choice her sister couldn't reconcile herself to. Emily's mother had then subsequently woven her own story about her sister's death to suit her own prejudices.

"From what little I know, I think it's safe to say your daughter's not your sister."

"Be that as it may, she's not thinking clearly. Obviously. Whether Michael—" She took a deep breath. "Whether he was right for her or not, three years is a big chunk of your life when you're that young. His cheating on her…" To his surprise, the older woman's eyes watered. "Emily's not like me. She has different…expectations. And she's still so young, as I said—"

"She's not a *child*, Mrs. Weber. And pardon me for saying this, but I find it very strange that you want so much to protect her when you threw her into that situation to begin with. How does that work, exactly?"

Her face colored, but give the woman props for standing her ground. "I'm not saying her father and I didn't make mistakes. Which is why I'm trying to head this one off at the pass now—"

"There's nothing to head off. There never was. While I'm hardly going to get specific about…things between Emily and me, we both knew going in exactly what the expectations were. Or weren't. Trust me, I didn't seduce her. Or make promises I had no intention of keeping. I was at least honest. And I'd put out my own eye before treating her like the man you picked for her did. *My* mistake…" Colin sucked in a breath. "My mistake was in not realizing how vulnerable we *both* were. And I cannot tell you how sorry I am for that. Especially since…since I care very deeply for your daughter. *About* her. And because I care, I wouldn't dream of quashing her dreams. Or putting her in a situation that would only make her unhappy down the road."

"Exactly what she said you'd say," Margaret said.

And hell, yeah, that hurt, for a whole mess of reasons. Not the least of which was how well Emily knew him, even after such a short time. "The point is, whether you came over here to warn me off, or somehow fix things between me and Emily…" His head wagged. "The first is moot, and the second isn't up to you. And never would be. Because nobody can make things work for someone else simply because they want them to. No matter what the motive. The fact is, Emily and I want different things. *Need* different things. And we're both mature enough to see that. Right now. Before we make any more mistakes than have already been made."

Margaret's eyes narrowed slightly. "One question—do you love her?"

Speaking of not pulling punches. "If I didn't," he said quietly, "I wouldn't be leaving tomorrow."

"Does she know that?"

"I'm going to say yes." Then he crossed his arms. "But my question to you is…what do you really want for her? Not for yourself. For *her*?"

Emily's mother slid off the stool, leaving her tea mostly undrunk. Her eyes welled again. "Happiness. That's all. Just…happiness."

"Then we're on the same page," Colin said, even as it felt like a knife was twisting in his gut. "Obviously you know your daughter a helluva lot better than I do, long-term. But you haven't been around her in the last few weeks, haven't seen…" He swallowed. "The way she smiles now…it's nothing like when she first got here. Like…like she's *whole*, finally. And finally herself. You really want her to be happy? Then trust that she'll figure out whatever she needs to figure out, in her own good time. Even if that's in some dinky little Southwest town."

"Which my niece hated. Which I gather you were pretty keen to leave, too—"

"Oh, I don't know. Deanna seems pretty content here these days, don't you think? And my reasons for leaving back then…" His mouth pushed up at the corners. "Oddly, they were—are—not unlike your daughter's for wanting to stay. Home's a funny thing, you know? Some of us find it right where we were born, others…maybe not so much. Maybe I don't feel Whispering Pines gives me the opportunity to do what I feel I need to do, but that doesn't make it a bad town." His voice softened. "And my family…they're good people, all of 'em. They'll keep an eye on Emily. Make sure she's never lonely. Make sure she's…safe."

This last part he said through a throat so thick he wasn't sure how he he'd gotten the words out.

Emily's mother was quiet for a long moment before she said, "Guess you've given me a lot to think about." She started for the door, then twisted back, her brow furrowed. "I can tell you're a good man, Colin. From my experience, those are pretty rare these days." A tiny smile flicked across her mouth. "And I wish you well. I really do."

Took a good five minutes after she left for Colin's heart to stop hammering in his chest.

Emily didn't see her mother again until the following morning, when she'd gone into the kitchen to make herself coffee and the older woman sat at the kitchen table, dressed and perfectly coiffed, lying in wait. Or sitting, in this case. In an ideal world, she would have acted as though everything was perfectly fine, that her mother's presence was neither here nor there, that whatever the woman had to say—and Emily had no doubt she had plenty—would simply bounce off her as harmlessly as Nerf bullets.

In reality, however, she hadn't slept worth spit, her heart was in tatters, and the anticipation alone of whatever was about to fall from her mother's freshly reddened lips made her feel about five again.

Except she wasn't. And even though Emily still wouldn't call herself fierce, she was a survivor, wasn't she? Hell, she'd lived through not only the mortification of having to let several hundred people know that, nope, sorry, there wouldn't be a wedding—not to mention the extra-added-value mortification of everyone knowing *why*—but the indignity of a broken heart brought on by nothing other than her own foolishness. Not that loving Colin was wrong, but letting things get as far as they had…

Just hand over the dumbass medal and be done with it.

So not really in the mood to chat with dear old mom right now.

"Everyone else is gone," Mother said, patting the space at the table next to her. "Although on Josh's recommendation I went into town early to pick up some breakfast things at that diner. Annie's. Since we all know I do not cook. Although I nearly killed myself in that truck—it's been a million years since I drove stick."

Her mug clutched to her chest, Emily stood frozen to the spot in front of the coffeemaker, letting the steam open her pores. Her brain cells. She wasn't sure who this woman was, but sure as shootin' it wasn't the one who'd given birth to her. By C-section after a twenty-eight-hour labor, she'd been told more times than she could remember. However…she was hungry, and Annie's churros and breakfast burritos were the stuff of magic. So she sat—her mother had already set a plate—and took a burrito, not sure what to say. Or do. Or think.

"You were already asleep when I got back from Colin's last night," her mother began, and Emily's head whipped around.

"What?"

"I peeked into your room, but you were out like a light—"

"No, the Colin bit." Although she hadn't been asleep, she'd been playing possum. The burrito forgotten, Emily's brows crashed. "You went to see him? Why on earth—?"

"Because I'm a meddling old biddy who's absolutely no good at keeping her nose out of everyone's business. Most notably yours. Eat up, honey, those things are disgusting when they're cold. Anyway, you'll be relieved to know he set me straight. About your relationship. About more than that, actually," she said, her mouth turning down at the corners. "But that's… Never mind." Her mother's eyes met hers. "What a remarkable young man. Youngish, anyway. He loves you, you know. Maybe even more than you love him. How on earth that happened in a few weeks is beyond me. But apparently it did."

As if there was any way in hell she'd be able to eat now. Although whether Colin had admitted his feelings or her mother had leaped to her own conclusions, who knew? But since she'd done her own leaping not that long ago, this didn't come as a surprise. What had, however, shocked her expensive, bought-for-the-honeymoon-that-never-happened designer panties right off her butt was her mother's calm acceptance of all of it.

Although since it was all a moot point, that might account for the calm. However…

"None of which changes the fact that I'm staying."

Her mother lifted her own mug to her lips. "Oh, I know."

"And…you're okay with that?"

"I will be. Once I unstick my head from my butt." As Emily sat there, more or less in shock, her mother said, "Colin made me realize a few things, not the least of which is that you have to live your own life. *Deserve* to live your own life. And that I can't fix what's wrong with my life by trying to manipulate yours. Or use you as some sort of shield between me and your father. But more than that…" Her eyes watered. "Keeping you close won't bring my sister back. And Deanna swears Kathryn was happy here. Most of the time, anyway."

Although Emily hadn't been around her aunt enough to be all that aware of the mental illness that robbed her of a good chunk of her adulthood, she, too, had heard enough to believe that the good outweighed the bad, even near the end. "It definitely seems that way. But I don't—"

Her generally undemonstrative mother wrapped a cool hand around Emily's wrist. "I've let fear color things for much too long, honey. Fear for you, especially, that history might repeat itself. So I've promised myself I won't do that anymore. And now I'm promising you."

Finally, Emily pinched off a chunk of the burrito and stuffed it into her mouth. "And I'm supposed to believe that?"

Her mother sighed. "It won't be easy—old dogs and all that—but I'm going to try. Although…" Her head tilted. "Maybe you should try to make Colin stay? Or go with him…?"

"Mother. Really?"

She sniffed. "Dignity is overrated, you know."

"Reality, however, isn't. All done with the fairy tale, Mom. Not really cut out for this dream-chasing business."

Another breath left her mother's lungs, but she nodded. "Well. I'm going back today. To face the mess that is my own life and leave you to live yours in peace."

Her throat closed around the bite in her mouth, Emily could only nod. Although fortunately her mother waited for her to swallow before saying, "That doesn't mean, however, that I'm not hoping either you or Colin change your mind."

A harsh laugh tumbled from Emily's mouth, and her mother shrugged. "I might be able to change how I act, but that doesn't mean I can change who I am. I'm so sorry, honey," she whispered, her eyes filling again. "Really and truly. For letting my own will blind me to how perfect you are, just as you are. When I think how I almost lost you…" Her face paled. "Or am I jumping the gun about that, too? Have I totally screwed this up?"

"Well, you might've come really close," Emily said with a small smile, "but…" Instead of finishing her sentence, she stood to wrap her startled mother in the first hug they'd shared since Emily was a little girl. What was more startling, however, was that her mother returned it.

And, *yanno*, that left her feeling pretty darn fierce.

Despite an ache in the center of her chest she doubted would ever completely go away. Because Michael—a dime a dozen, those types. Colin, however…

He was a Talbot. And those guys were priceless.

"When's your flight?" she said, sitting back down.

"At three. Josh said he'd take me into Albuquerque. Since I might've lucked out in finding an Uber driver to schlep me all the way out here, getting one to take me back—"

"Forget it, I'll drive you."

Her mother smiled, her eyes twinkling. "Making sure I actually leave?" she asked, and Emily laughed, only to then feel a lump rise in her throat.

"No," she said, surprised to find herself fighting tears. "Because the ride will give us another couple of hours together." And her mother smiled, her own eyes just as glittery.

Colin pulled up in front of his parents' house, not sure whether he was more relieved or sorry that his dad's truck wasn't in the driveway. His mother, however, greeted him at the door…along with the sounds of several high-pitched voices winnowing through the house from the small backyard. Zach and Mallory's kids, he remembered—his parents were babysitting while his brother and his new wife enjoyed a short honeymoon.

"Your father had to go into Taos for a doctor's appointment," she said, standing aside so he could come in. "A standard follow-up, that's all. Nothing to worry about. He'll be back soon, I imagine. So. To what do I owe the pleasure?"

A simple question, one that shouldn't have made the back of his throat clog, his eyes burn. But between his father not being there and the sounds of his nephews...

Not to mention other things...

"Catching a plane in a few," he said. "Figured I'd come by before I left."

His mother went immediately into Mom Alert—narrowed eyes, set mouth, that slight shake of her head that said she knew damn well there was more to it than that.

"Kind of sudden, isn't it?" she said, heading toward the kitchen and clearly expecting him to follow.

"You knew I was leaving after the wedding," he said, which earned him an even sharper glance.

"Not right after, I didn't. I mean, I figured we'd have a little warning. That you'd at least come over for dinner or something, say goodbye properly."

The barely masked hurt in her eyes killed him nearly as much as what he'd seen in Emily's the night before, when they both realized—and admitted—what they were really feeling. And that it didn't make a lick of difference.

"I know, I'm sorry. But a new assignment came up suddenly. Since the wedding was over, I figured I might as well jump on it before somebody else does."

Not entirely a lie. Another editor had dangled something different in front of him, wondering if he'd consider doing a human interest piece on how changing energy options were affecting residents of one area of the country. Not his usual focus, but something that'd been tickling the back of his brain for a while, anyway. And if nothing else it provided him with a viable, and reasonable, excuse to leave. And one nobody would question.

His mother crossed her arms. "So what're you running from this time? As if I couldn't guess."

Nobody but Mom, that was. "Excuse me?"

"Josh has a big mouth, God love him. Not to mention he's worried about you."

"Why on earth—?" Mom gave him a don't-talk-stupid look that halfway made Colin regret stopping here on the way to the airport. She glanced out the kitchen window to check on the boys, then turned back to him, her gaze managing to be both sharp and soft at the same time. A particular talent of hers, as it happened.

"Whatever's going on with you and Emily—or not— that's between you and her. And I've got no issues with your devotion to your work. I know how it feels, finding something that feeds something deep inside you. A lot of people never do, so you've got a leg up there, at least. However…"

She closed the space between them to clamp her hands around his arms, her expression twisting him inside out. "What worries me," she said gently, "is that I'm guessing you haven't been entirely honest with yourself, about why you came back. Because you and I both know you could've worked on that book anywhere. You didn't have to do it here. Especially considering how you and your daddy left things all those years ago. But it's not that easy to turn our backs on our roots, is it? Especially if we haven't set down new ones somewhere else."

Now he was really regretting stopping by. "And again— where is this coming from?"

"The look on your face, for one thing. Which is not the look of somebody excited about getting back to his chosen life."

When he didn't answer—couldn't—Mom returned to the window, chuckling at something the kids were doing, her sleeveless blouse showing off arms as toned as those of a much younger woman. "You know, one of the hardest things we all have to learn is that it's okay to change our minds." She looked back at him. "That there's no shame in admitting we were wrong."

And how terrible a son would he be for blowing off his own mother? Although, come to think of it, probably no worse than he'd already been. Except the thing was, he wasn't that kid anymore. Besides which, being back here had not only shoved his face into everything he'd given up, but everything he'd refused for so long to admit he wanted. His mother was right—he'd wanted to return to his roots, to reground himself. Badly.

Except unfortunately this wasn't only about him. Not anymore.

"You're way too smart for your own good, you know that?"

Mom snorted. "You're not telling me anything I don't know," she said, and Colin smiled. Then cupped the back of his head.

"You're right, I'm not happy about this. But…" He pushed out a dry laugh. "I'm not running away. I swear. It's more that… I'm deliberately getting out of someone else's way."

"Oh, sweetie…" Tears gleamed in his mother's eyes. "You're in love with the girl, aren't you?"

From out front, he heard his father's truck door slam shut. Clearing his throat, Colin dug the rental's keys out of his pocket. Tried a smile. "Close enough. The thing is, though, I know what would happen if I stayed. What we'd both want to happen. Except Emily's right where I was ten years ago, just beginning to find her own footing, to figure out who she is, what she wants. She needs the space to figure that out.

But if I stick around—" He shrugged. "*Space* isn't something you get much of in a small town."

"And maybe you're not giving either of you enough credit—"

"For what? *Listening* to her? Paying attention to what she needs? You and Dad…you showed us by example that selfishness has no place in a working relationship. And I can't…*won't*…" He swallowed painfully past the knot in his throat, then glanced up at the kitchen clock. "Sorry, I need to get going or I'm gonna miss my plane—"

"You're leaving? Already?"

At his father's voice, Colin turned. And man, seeing the look in his father's eyes…at that moment he hated himself, hated the situation, hated life, pretty much.

"Something came up, I…"

"It's okay, son," Dad said, even though he was clearly fighting off disappointment. "It's not like we expected you to hang around. As it is…well." Grinning, he clapped Colin's shoulder, then hauled him against his still-broad chest. "We're grateful you hung around as long as you did."

"So am I, Dad," Colin said quietly. "Really."

"I know." His father let go, managing a piss-poor smile that tore Colin up inside. "You have a good trip, you hear?"

Then his mother also yanked him into a hard hug and kissed his cheek before holding him at arm's length, her mouth twisted to one side. "I swear, every one of you boys has a head harder than granite. Can't imagine where you get that from."

"I'm gonna say both of you," Colin said, and she harmlessly swatted his chest before they both followed him out to the front door. When he got there, though, he turned, his hand on the knob. "I will be back, though. I promise."

Dad crossed his arms. "Sooner rather than later, I hope."

"Sure thing," he said, then got out of there before somebody called him on his lie.

The ride down to Albuquerque had given Emily and her mother an opportunity to talk to—rather than at—each other in a way they never had before. So much so that their hug before Margaret went through security left Emily far more torn up than she would have expected even a week ago. Not that they'd magically become BFFs or anything, but at least they'd arrived at some sort of understanding of where they were each coming from. As though they were equals, even, she thought as she got on the escalator to go down to the lower level and out to the parking garage. Not to mention that, for the first time in years, she really *felt* her mother loved her. That was something—

At the bottom of the escalator, she lost her breath. Because, yep, that was Colin striding across the vast, tiled expanse toward her, his camera bag draped over his shoulder as he stared at his phone, gracefully dodging the smattering of passengers this time of day. Meaning he probably wouldn't even see her, if she kept going—

His head snapped up as if she'd called to him, a frown giving way to a dozen other emotions as he changed course and headed toward her, his mouth curved in a slight smile. He hadn't shaved, she could now see. Or slept, she was guessing.

"Hey," he said softly when he reached her, and Emily nearly melted from how badly she wanted to touch him. "What are you…?"

"Just dropped off my mother."

"Really?" He glanced around, as though expecting to see her. "She left already?"

"Yeah. She…" Emily gave her head a sharp little shake, then shrugged. "Yeah. She, um, told me she went to see you."

She couldn't read his expression. "Really."

"But not what you two discussed. And I didn't ask. Although she did leave, so…thanks?"

His gaze met hers again, and everything inside her trembled, glowed, with the memory of his touch, rough and tender and almost hesitant…those eyes locked on hers, anything *but* hesitant. His smile incrementally grew. "I'm surprised you let her live."

Emily almost laughed. "Things were definitely a little dicey there for a minute. But you know what? She's always gonna be who she is, nothing I can do about that. What I can control is whether or not she gets to me. And those days are over."

Colin's smile broadened. "So she couldn't talk you into going back to DC?"

The obvious pride in his voice, his eyes… Oh, dear *God*, just kill her now. "As if," she said, and he laughed, but it didn't sound normal. Or maybe that was her hearing.

"When's your flight?" she asked.

"Not for a couple of hours yet. I like to get to airports early. Although I forget it's not that big a deal here."

"Not really, no." Yeesh, could this conversation be any more inane? Could her heart be hammering any harder? Or splintering into any more pieces?

"Where are you headed?"

"Coal country. Or what used to be. Kentucky, West Virginia. A piece on how things have changed there."

"A new direction for you, isn't it?"

"Maybe. Or not." He shifted the camera bag. "It's still about the people." A smile ghosted around his mouth. "It's always about the people."

Don't get sucked in, she wanted to say. But she knew

that wasn't possible, not for this man. Any more than it would be for her.

"Take care," she whispered, and he nodded.

"I will. Promise."

"Well. I guess…"

"Sure. It was—"

"I know." Crap. She was going to cry. "Um…" She swallowed so hard she nearly choked. "Have a good trip."

"Thanks."

She nodded, then walked quickly away, her eyes burning so badly she could barely see—

"Em?"

Muttering an obscenity under her breath, she turned, helpless to do anything save watch Colin march toward her again, even more helpless to resist when he somehow shifted everything aside to take her face in his hands and lower his mouth to hers for a kiss that was a desperate, mournful meeting of mouths and tongues and souls and hearts…until he broke the kiss to press his lips against her forehead before taking off again, his long legs eating up the tiled floor as he strode to the escalators.

And didn't look back as he ascended.

Emily, however, watched until he was out of sight, although whether from a false sense of hope or a hitherto unknown masochistic streak, she had no idea. And she wondered, gripping her purse's shoulder strap like a lifeline, how a life decision that only the day before had made her feel empowered and independent and all grownup now made her feel like a horse stall that hadn't been mucked out since the dawn of time.

Have a fling, they said. *It'll be fun*, they said.

You can handle it, they said.

Except if "they" were here in front of her right now? She'd slap those bitches silly.

Chapter Twelve

Twisting off the beer's cap, Colin shoved aside the patio door to the bland Midwestern condo he'd used as little more than a mailing address for the past ten years, letting the humid June air—not to mention a swarm of gnats—grab at his face before he dropped into some sorry old webbed chair he'd picked up for a couple bucks when the old lady downstairs died and her kids sold off all her stuff. The apartment wasn't horrible by any means, the kind of place he knew he could leave for long periods without worrying overmuch about break-ins. Not to mention maintenance. The rent was reasonable, the neighbors as oblivious to his comings and goings as he was to theirs, the location almost ideal for getting anywhere else with a minimum of connecting flights. It was also fairly quiet, especially since the college kids had moved out. And if it didn't exactly feel like home… Again—not here that often. It was…enough.

Or had been, anyway.

Because for the first time, when he'd gotten back from his assignment late yesterday afternoon, instead of he and the condo greeting each other with bored indifference, Colin had felt a definite pang of annoyance. Like when you suddenly realized the girlfriend you'd stayed with out of habit more than anything wasn't who you really wanted to be with anymore. That, suddenly, you wanted more. *Needed* more. Even if you didn't know what, exactly, that *more* was.

Only—he glanced across the reasonably green, reasonably kept courtyard toward the bank of balconies that looked exactly like his, save for slight variations in grills and doodads—who was he kidding? He knew exactly what he wanted. Who he wanted.

And he'd known it long before he'd gotten on that plane a few weeks ago.

Before he'd gotten naked with a woman who'd stripped him bare long before that night.

Before his mother sent him that text, a few days after he left—

His phone buzzed, startling him. Colin picked it up off the also-crappy glass table by the chair, frowning at Levi's number. He doubted whether any of his brothers had the slightest clue why he'd left. Although if he'd bothered to tell them why he'd really returned to his hometown to begin with, they might have.

"Figured I should let you know your newest niece is here," his younger brother said, the obvious grin in his voice making Colin smile even over the fresh stab to his heart.

"She is? That's terrific."

"A relief, is what it is. Kid took her sweet time making her appearance. The due date was nearly two weeks ago.

Then after all that she came flying out like a greased pig. Although don't tell Val I said that." He laughed. "Mom barely had a chance to catch her. A little blondie. Like her mama."

Trying to ignore the tug, Colin said, "What's her name?"

He heard Levi clear his throat. "Hope," he said quietly. "Val's suggestion. Like I was gonna say no, right?"

His own throat tightening, Colin glanced back out into the green space between the buildings, right when a young family walked by with a toddler streaking toward the complex's little playground, and an infant in a stroller, black eyes wide in a gleaming brown face. Newish residents, he guessed, since he'd never seen them before. The dad apparently said something to get a rise out of his wife…and succeeded, judging from her squawk, followed by a gentle smack on his muscled arm, their blended laughter. They caught Colin looking at them. He grinned and waved; they waved back, and a thousand thoughts seemed to take flight inside Colin's head, a swarm of locusts intent on devouring everything in their path.

Like all those good intentions that seemed to make less sense with every passing day.

Aka the masks for his fears.

"I'd like to… I want to come see her," he said into the phone, clearly startling his brother. "If it's not too soon. I don't want to mess things up if you're still trying to get settled—"

"No! I mean, not at all, anytime's good. That'd be great." Levi paused. "But I figured you'd be busy, you know. With your work and stuff. Like always."

"Like I was when Zach's boys were born, you mean."

A moment of silence preceded, "I wasn't here, either, being in the service—"

"You had an excuse, Lev. Me? Not so much. And I know Zach never understood, not really." He pushed out a dry laugh. "Hell, I didn't fully understand myself, so why would anybody else? Anyway…not sure when I'll get there—"

"No hurry, bro." His brother chuckled. "Kid's not going anywhere. Although, even setting aside whatever it is you do…that's not the only reason I'm surprised you're coming home."

Yeah, Colin wondered how long it'd take Levi to get around to that.

"Not that I'm about to get into the middle of that mess," his brother continued. "Or whatever you want to call it. But let me say this, and then I'm done, I swear—I can tell you from experience that sometimes the one thing that seems to make the least sense is exactly what you need to do. You got that?" At Colin's snort, his brother added, "So you want me to give Emily a heads-up, or no?"

"I'm only coming to see the kid, I…" He shoved out a breath. Like anybody would believe that. "Do whatever you think best, okay?"

Then, on another breath, Colin disconnected the call. Hell, at this point he was way past worrying about anything making sense. Right now—especially when faced with the prospect of seeing the woman he hadn't been able to stop thinking about from the minute he walked away from her in the airport—all he wanted was to know, and do, whatever was right. For both of them.

He only hoped to hell he figured that out before he balled things up even worse. Although he wasn't counting on it. Not at all. Because it was still too soon, for Emily. Wasn't it? Really, had anything changed? It wasn't as if they were somehow different people now than when he'd left…

Except without trying, what was the point of living?

Something he had the definite feeling nobody would agree with more than the woman who'd made him realize that *more* had been right under his nose all along. Because everything he wanted, and could be, was right in that dinky little New Mexico town.

Because making a difference had nothing to do with where you were, but what you did.

And who you did it for.

Still watching the little family, Colin tapped his phone against his chin, then brought up his mother's text again. One of her favorite Bible verses, he remembered.

For where your treasure is, there your heart will be also.

A promise, he realized. For everyone.

Even him.

Colin could practically hear God's sigh of relief, that *finally* he'd caught on.

Carefully rocking the prettiest little baby girl in the whole world, Emily barely heard the doorbell ring over toddler Risa's clattering her mama's pie tins against the kitchen's tiled floor. Of course, then Levi and Val's hound dog, Radar, started baying his head off, so it's not as if she could've missed that "somebody's at the door, woman, *fer* God's sake!"

So much for poor Val trying to get a nap, Emily thought as she shoved aside the dog to open the door, a task made far more difficult by the toddler's clinging to her legs.

"Hey," Colin said, and every bit of spit in Emily's mouth evaporated and every one of the pep talks she'd given herself since she last saw him, about how this was for the best and she was strong and happy and good on her own, *blahblahblahbityblah*, flew right out the window. Then he frowned at what must have been her gobsmacked expression. "I'm guessing Levi didn't tell you I was coming."

At least she thought that's what he said. Hard to tell over the pounding in her ears and Risa's shrieks of joy as she launched herself at her uncle's knees and Radar's *roo-rooing*. Because the dog was high on life, basically.

"Who's that?" Val said behind her, in jeans and a floppy, sloppy shirt but otherwise giving no indication whatsoever she'd popped out a kid two days ago. "Colin!" The blonde zoomed across the room to throw her arms around her brother-in-law, her long ponytail swinging against her back as she laughed. "Oh, my god! I certainly didn't expect you to show up!"

"Surprise," Colin said quietly, his gaze hooking Emily's as he said, "I heard there's a new Talbot in town."

Val pivoted, took one look at Emily's still-gobsmacked expression, pivoted back to Colin and said, "Who you can see later. First things first." Then she pried her new daughter out of Emily's arms, called the dog and her little girl and steered the whole lot out back.

A moment before Colin stepped inside, cupped Emily's face in his hands and kissed her as though his life depended on it. Or hers, maybe.

"Where's Spud?" he asked when they came up for air, and Emily sputtered a laugh.

"At the cabin," she said. "Where we live now. He's gotten so big, you won't even recognize him—"

"We need to hash out a few things," Colin said, his hands still cradling her face, all warm and firm and goose bumps–inducing…his mouth still right there, much too close for rational thought. Somehow, she squeaked out a little "Okay" before he laughed—oh, Lord, did she love that laugh!—and took her hand to lead her to his brother's living room, where he shoved aside a layer of little girl toys from the scarred sofa and pulled her down onto his lap. And Emily had no idea what was going on, and frankly she didn't care, because she'd never been as happy as she was right at that moment. Since, you know, she doubted he was going to say "So here's the thing…" and get up and leave.

And if none of that made any sense from a practical standpoint…

Screw it.

Colin tucked her against his chest, his cheek on the top of her head, and said, "Okay, so here's the thing… What's so funny?"

"Nothing," she said, swallowing her laughter and snuggling closer. "So what's the thing?"

He was quiet for a moment, stroking her back, chuckling when Val's little gray tiger cat jumped up beside him and promptly settled in, purring. He stroked the blissful beast for another couple of seconds, then said, "I have no idea how—or even if—this could work between us. Or even if it should. But this pansy-ass pussyfooting deal is for the birds."

Frowning, Emily sat up to look into those pretty, tortured green eyes. "Oh, yeah?"

Matching her frown, Colin sighed, then linked their hands on her lap. "I told myself I'd left to give you space. That the timing sucked, I didn't want to crowd you…you name it, I trotted it out."

"Not to mention," she carefully ventured, "I want to stay here and you don't."

One side of his mouth pushed up. "Except…" He lifted her hand, brought it to his mouth, then tucked it against his chest. "I do. Want to stay. At least, to make Whispering Pines my home base." A sad smile curved his lips. "My *home*. Again. See, the plan *had* been to shove my pride aside enough to finally admit that I've wanted to come home for a while. That when all was said and done, this was the only place I ever felt as though I belonged. Only…" His eyes moist, he lifted a hand to brush her hair away from her face. "Only then you happened."

"And I totally messed up your plan?"

That got a soft laugh. "Sort of. But not the way I'd convinced myself you had. I really was thinking of you, I swear. That you were on the rebound, that you didn't need complications. Which means that's something we still have to work out. If you want. *But*…"

He paused, his gaze fixed for several moments on the space in front of him before he pushed out a breath. "But even before I left, I had to admit that your issues were a convenient excuse."

"For?"

His eyes locked in hers. "For me avoiding mine."

Emily went very still, half honored that Colin was about to really open up to her, half petrified of what that might mean. Except she once again reminded herself…he was *here*. And that the way he'd kissed her…

Breathe, she told herself. *Just…breathe.*

"I was so sure it'd be safe here," he said. "That *I'd* be safe, from anything even remotely like temptation. That this…that it'd be not only a safe haven for when I need a break from my work, but—" He pressed their entwined hands to his chest. "But that my heart would be safe here, too," he said quietly, and Emily's cracked. "That I could enjoy my brothers' families without having to…"

He swallowed.

"Be afraid for your own," Emily said gently.

Tears shimmered in his eyes when he let their gazes meet. "It's not that I don't want a family or children, Em.

It's that, after everything I've seen, the idea of losing them…"

"I know," she whispered. "I do."

"*But* I'm far, far more afraid of losing the best thing that's ever happened to me." He let go of her hand to cup her jaw, his fingers forked through her hair. "Which would be you."

Emily kept her gaze hooked in his for several seconds before she pushed up from his lap, earning a pissed *chir-rup?* from the cat.

"Em…?"

"So what happened to logic?" she said, not facing him, and Colin laughed.

"Don't know," he said. "Don't care. And if it's still too soon, I'll understand. But…" He got to his feet and closed the gap between them to wrap her up from behind and whisper in her hair, "How could I not love the woman who made me face everything I've ignored for years? Who's made me figure out who I am? What I *truly* want?"

Emily shut her eyes, by now sure they could hear her heart thundering as far north as Wyoming. Then she turned in his arms, all that hope in his eyes knocking clean out of her what little breath she had left. "Same here," she somehow got out. "But I haven't changed my mind about wanting children, Colin. If you still don't—"

"You know what I finally realized? That there's prob-ably not a single parent alive who doesn't worry about something happening to their kids. At least sometimes." His gaze softened. "That's not the same as not wanting them. Even if I'd told myself that for so long I almost—almost—believed it. And to have them with you… I get almost dizzy just thinking about it," he said, and she laughed, only to suck in a deep breath.

"And your work? Your calling? You know no way in hell would I ever interfere with that, right?"

A good two, three seconds passed before Colin said, "I do. But I promise you, even if I can't always be around, I'd always be here for you. Be in your camp. Because you're my treasure," he said, and she absolutely melted.

"Crap," Emily muttered, then snagged a tissue out of the box on the end table to loudly blow her nose. "You're my treasure, too, you big g-goofball…" Then, apparently no longer capable of coherent speech, she made some strange, strangled little sound, and Colin pulled her close again, his heartbeat steady against her ear…and then their mouths met, and… *Oh, my, yes.*

Yes.

Then, after what seemed like an eternity of some very satisfying spit swapping, they simply stood wrapped in each other's arms, listening to Val and the kids outside, an overloud dove cooing outside the living room window. Until at last Colin said, "From the moment I saw you standing on the porch with the damned dog, I was a goner. By the time we left Zach's after getting Spud fixed up…it—you—felt right. I mean, crazy, earth-shatteringly right. And that pull, that rightness…"

"I know," she whispered. "Me, too."

"But—"

"I know," she repeated, snuggling closer.

Chuckling, he kissed her head. "Forgive me?"

"I'll think about it."

He paused, then whispered, "Marry me?"

Her head jerked back so hard her neck snapped. "Are you serious?"

"Hey. If the universe went to this much trouble to throw the two of us together…"

Had to admit, the man had a point. Because actually, the timing couldn't have been any more perfect—

"But only if you want to," he said.

And Val yelled, "Oh, for heaven's sake!" from the kitchen, making them both jump. "Put the poor man out of his misery! Not to mention me!"

Laughing, Emily linked her hands around Colin's neck. "Oh, I want to, all right," she said, and he blew out a very relieved breath. Then she grinned. "Although my poor mother will have kittens."

Colin's smile melted her heart. "And we'll find homes for them all," he said, after which Emily discovered exactly how hard it was to kiss somebody when you couldn't stop smiling.

Epilogue

"**Y**ou nervous, son?"

Colin smiled over at his father, feeling such warmth toward the older man it nearly took his breath. He looked away, into the cloudless fall sky stretching above the Vista's front acreage, where a couple dozen folding chairs had been set up for the simple ceremony to follow. Just family and a few friends. Emily's parents, in from DC. They'd separated, although to hear Emily tell it this was not only not a bad thing, but long overdue. Sounded to him like his almost mother-in-law had finally grown a pair, frankly. In no small part due to her daughter's example. His smile broadening, he met Sam's gaze again.

"Not at all."

Dressed almost exactly like Colin in a Western-style shirt, tucked into "good" jeans, and a silver bolo tie, Dad clapped Colin's shoulder, muttered, "Oh, what the hell?" then pulled him into a brief, hard hug. They'd probably talked more in the past few months than in the whole eighteen years prior to Colin's leaving for college. Funny, the way adulthood had of smoothing out the edges. Especially when those edges had been far more on one side than Colin might've wanted to admit. His father was a good man. Hardheaded, maybe, but good. But the most important thing was that he adored Emily. Both his parents did. As did she, them. Hell, even her snooty mother had warmed up to Billie. Although this was not a surprise, knowing his mother.

What had been a surprise—or maybe not, come to think of it—was how easily Colin had settled back into life in Whispering Pines, with his family, the community. How between assignments he'd found a renewed sense of purpose in working alongside Mallory in her therapy facility, helping both kids and adults with various challenges find theirs. Seeing those smiles...

Because there was no *small* way to make a difference, was there?

Then people were taking seats, trying to corral children long enough for the minister to do what they were paying him for. And a minute after that his bride was coming down the aisle, her estranged parents on either side, looking resigned to the inevitable if nothing else. Emily, though...

Colin's throat clogged. Emily had adamantly refused to let Margaret Weber anywhere near the wedding preparations, such as they'd been. In fact, most of the decorations bore the distinct hallmarks of a pair of nine-year-olds with more love and enthusiasm than skill. Emily's dress, though, had been a secret from everyone—she hadn't even let Deanna go into Albuquerque with her to get it. And now he couldn't catch his breath at how freaking gorgeous she was in the simple, shimmery ivory dress, her long hair loosely wound around a few little flowers. The woman simply couldn't not do classy, that was all there was to it.

Even in the midst of a woefully outdated foreman's cabin, or mucking out a horse stall…or traipsing through a mud-bogged Central American village with a batch of chattering children clinging to her hands.

Still, Colin was barely aware of what she was wearing for her radiant smile, the same one she'd given to all those children, and anyone else who crossed her path—brighter than the late September sun flashing through the yellowing cottonwoods. Then their hands and eyes were joined, along with their hearts, and the minister pronounced them husband and wife…

And his bride laughed into his eyes, and he was finally, forever, home.

* * * * *

Find the other Talbot brothers' love stories in previous books in Karen Templeton's
WED IN THE WEST *miniseries:*

THE RANCHER'S EXPECTANT CHRISTMAS (Josh)
BACK IN THE SADDLE (Zach)
A SOLDIER'S PROMISE (Levi)

Available now from Harlequin Special Edition!

COMING NEXT MONTH FROM

HARLEQUIN®

SPECIAL EDITION

Available February 21, 2017

#2533 FORTUNE'S SECOND-CHANCE COWBOY
The Fortunes of Texas: The Secret Fortunes • by Marie Ferrarella
Young widow Chloe Fortune Eliot falls for Chance Howell, an ex-soldier with PTSD, but will their fear of another heartbreak stop them both from seizing a second chance at love?

#2534 JUST A LITTLE BIT MARRIED
The Bachelors of Blackwater Lake • by Teresa Southwick
Rose Tucker is a single woman with a failing business. Or so she thinks. Then her ex, Lincoln Hart, shows up with an offer for her design services...and the bombshell that a paperwork glitch makes them a little bit married.

#2535 KISS ME, SHERIFF!
The Men of Thunder Ridge • by Wendy Warren
Even as Willa Holmes vows not to risk loving again after a tragedy, she finds herself the subject of a hot pursuit by local sheriff Derek Neel. Can she escape the loving arm of the law? Does she even want to?

#2536 THE MARINE MAKES HIS MATCH
Camden Family Secrets • by Victoria Pade
Kinsey Madison has a strict policy about dating military men: she won't. Of course that means she can team up with Lieutenant Colonel Sutter Knightlinger to get his widowed mother settled and Kinsey in contact with her new family without risking her heart...right?

#2537 PREGNANT BY MR. WRONG
The McKinnels of Jewell Rock • by Rachael Johns
When anonymous advice columnist and playboy Quinn McKinnel receives a letter from Pregnant by Mr. Wrong, he recognizes the sender as Bailey Sawyer, his one-night-stand, and has to decide whether to simply fess up or win over the mother of his child.

#2538 A FAMILY UNDER THE STARS
Sugar Falls, Idaho • by Christy Jeffries
On a "glamping" trip for her magazine, Charlotte Folsom has a fling with her guide, Alex Russell. But back in Sugar Falls, they keep running into each other, and their respective families fill a void neither knew was missing. Will Charlotte and Alex be too stubborn to see the forest for the trees?

YOU CAN FIND MORE INFORMATION ON UPCOMING HARLEQUIN® TITLES, FREE EXCERPTS AND MORE AT WWW.HARLEQUIN.COM.

HSECNM0217

SPECIAL EXCERPT FROM

HARLEQUIN

SPECIAL EDITION

*A young widow falls for Chance Howell, an ex-soldier
with PTSD, but will Chloe Fortune Elliott's discovery
that she's linked to the famous Fortune family destroy
their chance at a future together?*

*Read on for a sneak preview of
the next book in **THE FORTUNES OF TEXAS:
THE SECRET FORTUNES** miniseries,
FORTUNE'S SECOND-CHANCE COWBOY,
by USA TODAY bestselling author Marie Ferrarella.*

Chance knew he should just go. Normally, he would have.
But something was making him dig in his heels and stay.
He wanted to get something straight.

"Is this the kind of stuff you're going to be feeding
those boys?" he asked. "Stuff about slaying dragons?"

"No, this is the kind of 'stuff' I'm going to be using
in order to try to understand the boys," she said. "To help
them reconnect with the world."

He laughed drily. Still sounded like a bunch of mumbo
jumbo to him.

"Well, good luck with that," he told her, shaking
his head. "But if you ask me, a little hard work and a
little responsibility should help those boys do all the
reconnecting that they need."

"Hard work and responsibility," she repeated, as if he
had just quoted scripture. "Has it helped you?" Chloe
asked innocently.

His scowl deepened for a moment, and then he just

waved her words away. "Don't try getting inside my head, Chloe Elliott. There's nothing in it for you. I'm doing just fine just the way I am."

She suppressed a sigh. "Okay, as long as you're happy."

Happy? When was the last time he'd been happy? He couldn't remember.

"Happy's got nothing to do with it," Chance answered. "I'm my own man on my own terms, and that's all that really counts."

He felt himself losing his temper, and he didn't want to do that. Once things were said, they couldn't get unsaid, and a lot of damage could be done. He didn't want that to happen. Not with this woman.

"I'd better go find the boss. Graham said that he wanted to take me around the spread as soon as I stashed my gear."

She didn't want to be the reason he was late. "Then I guess you'd better get going."

"Yeah, I guess I'd better." With that, he crossed back to the door.

He walked out feeling that there were things left unspoken. A great many things. But then, maybe it was better that way. He wasn't looking to have his head "shrunk" any more than it already was. Even if the lady doing the shrinking was nothing short of a knockout.

Some things, he reasoned, were just better off left alone.

Don't miss
FORTUNE'S SECOND-CHANCE COWBOY
by Marie Ferrarella,
available March 2017 wherever
Harlequin® Special Edition books and ebooks are sold.

www.Harlequin.com

HSEEXP0217

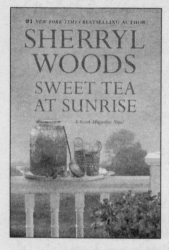

REQUEST YOUR FREE BOOKS!
2 FREE NOVELS PLUS 2 FREE GIFTS!

HARLEQUIN®

SPECIAL EDITION
Life, Love & Family

YES! Please send me 2 FREE Harlequin® Special Edition novels and my 2 FREE gifts (gifts are worth about $10). After receiving them, if I don't wish to receive any more books, I can return the shipping statement marked "cancel." If I don't cancel, I will receive 6 brand-new novels every month and be billed just $4.74 per book in the U.S. or $5.49 per book in Canada. That's a savings of at least 12% off the cover price! It's quite a bargain! Shipping and handling is just 50¢ per book in the U.S. and 75¢ per book in Canada.* I understand that accepting the 2 free books and gifts places me under no obligation to buy anything. I can always return a shipment and cancel at any time. Even if I never buy another book, the two free books and gifts are mine to keep forever.

235/335 HDN GH3Z

Name _____ (PLEASE PRINT) _____

Address _____ Apt. # _____

City _____ State/Prov. _____ Zip/Postal Code _____

Signature (if under 18, a parent or guardian must sign)

Mail to the **Reader Service:**
IN U.S.A.: P.O. Box 1867, Buffalo, NY 14240-1867
IN CANADA: P.O. Box 609, Fort Erie, Ontario L2A 5X3

Want to try two free books from another line?
Call 1-800-873-8635 or visit www.ReaderService.com.

* Terms and prices subject to change without notice. Prices do not include applicable taxes. Sales tax applicable in N.Y. Canadian residents will be charged applicable taxes. Offer not valid in Quebec. This offer is limited to one order per household. Not valid for current subscribers to Harlequin Special Edition books. All orders subject to credit approval. Credit or debit balances in a customer's account(s) may be offset by any other outstanding balance owed by or to the customer. Please allow 4 to 6 weeks for delivery. Offer available while quantities last.

Your Privacy—The Reader Service is committed to protecting your privacy. Our Privacy Policy is available online at www.ReaderService.com or upon request from the Reader Service.

We make a portion of our mailing list available to reputable third parties that offer products we believe may interest you. If you prefer that we not exchange your name with third parties, or if you wish to clarify or modify your communication preferences, please visit us at www.ReaderService.com/consumerchoice or write to us at Reader Service Preference Service, P.O. Box 9062, Buffalo, NY 14240-9062. Include your complete name and address.

HSE15